THE ILL-FATED
SCIENTIST

Syndicated columnist Tara Blunt knows her track record with men hasn't been stellar and now she's faced with four men in her life...and one of them might be a murderer.

Also by Alice Zogg

Stand-Alone Mysteries

Accidental Eyewitness
A Bet Turned Deadly

R. A. Huber Mysteries

Evil at Shore Haven
Guilty or Not
Murder at the Cubbyhole
Revamp Camp
Final Stop Albuquerque
The Fall of Optimum House
The Lonesome Autocrat
Tracking Backward
Turn the Joker Around
Reaching Checkmate

THE ILL-FATED SCIENTIST

ALICE ZOGG

aventine press

This book is a work of fiction.

Published by Aventine Press
55 East Emerson St.
Chula Vista CA 91911
www.aventinepress.com

ISBN: 978-1-59330-946-6

Library of Congress Control Number: 2018908327
Library of Congress Cataloging-in-Publication Data
THE ILL-FATED SCIENTIST/Alice Zogg
Printed in the United States of America

Here is another one for you, Wilfried

CREDITS

My thanks go to physics teacher David Platt, who answered scientific questions I had pertaining to physics mentioned in this book. If I still managed to get it wrong, any error relevant to that field is mine, not his. I would be at a loss without my daughter Franziska's proofreading skills. Thank you for taking the time to do this for your mom, over and over again. Gayle Bartos-Pool did an excellent editing job. I truly appreciate it, Gayle. My gratitude goes out to the members of the Los Angeles chapter of Sisters in Crime. Their support keeps me enthused about this thing called writing. Huntington Beach has become my spouse's and my home away from home. So it is only fitting that I chose its location for this work. By the same token, the setting research was effortless and did not involve traveling far. Wilfried, my husband, was easily persuaded to accompany me to a research outing on Balboa Island.

CHAPTER 1

Where to start? To be clear right from the beginning, I am not an author of books. My name is Tara Blunt. My métier as a syndicated columnist does not necessarily qualify me as being one. Still, I cannot ignore the events that put me smack in the middle of wickedness, and so I feel compelled to tell this story. I am writing it first and foremost for myself, needing to vent the morbid involvement, in order to draw the final curtain. Capturing any potential readers' interest in the process, I consider a bonus.

I guess the kickoff was when all hell broke loose on the day I finally landed an interview with Dr. Jake Unger. I had discovered that several scientists had entered a contest sponsored by a leading company in the soft drink industry named Tops & Associates. They were to come up with an eco-friendly cellulose-derived product that would replace all types of petroleum-based packaging. I was determined to interview these scientists about their entries.

Let me explain a little more about myself. I'm a 33-year-old light brunette who inherited my high cheekbones and long legs from Mom, a former model, and the ability to think logically from Dad, who is an engineer. I run my columns in multiple major national newspapers and magazines. On occasion, I also submit my work to specific targeted publications. Among other things, I am interested in environmental and conservation issues, and some of my articles reflect those subjects.

The task of talking to the scientists proved harder than I imagined. Initially, they all refused to see me. Since Jake Unger lived in my hometown of Huntington Beach in Southern California, I was persistent and contacted him several times. At long last, he agreed to meet me at the Starbuck's on Main Street for a short interview on that terrible Saturday morning of April 14 - - I presumed to get me off his back.

I judged him to be in his mid-to-late-thirties, tall and lanky, with a long skinny neck. I could not help comparing him to a giraffe as he awkwardly walked toward my table, cappuccino in hand. He was not a conversationalist at all. I had to drag every bit of information out of him, meager as it was. I learned that he had a master's degree in physics and first worked in a government-funded laboratory doing experimental research, then switched over to the private sector and became self-employed. I asked him how he could survive being self-employed with the cost of research projects coming out of his own pocket. He gave me a look of annoyance at my obvious ignorance but answered the question, informing me that he contracted with different companies, who in turn financed the research for the assignments. When prompted about his current project as participant in the contest, he became even more tongue-tied.

I asked, "Are you close to a breakthrough or have you already found a solution?"

"You might say that."

"But you won't talk about it?"

"Correct." And I was surprised that he opened up enough to add, "Deadline for submission is a week from today. Perhaps I'll tell you afterward."

No wonder the contestants did not grant me interviews. They were all pressured for time, I thought. Aloud I said, "Dr. Unger, I take it that you are passionate about environmental issues."

"Not really," he admitted.

"So why did you enter the contest?"

"The prize money is substantial, and the prestige accompanied with it, welcome."

"Where do you work?"

"I use the separate guest house in back of my home as a lab."

"May I have a look?" I asked.

"Why?"

"Just curious. Besides, if you win the contest, I'll not only write a generous column about you and your discovery, which will appear in numerous major newspapers and professional magazines, but I'll add a photo of your lab to boot."

He thought this over and then reluctantly agreed to let me have a peek. We settled on 4:30 that same afternoon.

CHAPTER 2

My apartment is located in central Huntington Beach, about five miles inland. Jake Unger's house was near the ocean and a few blocks from Main Street. His was one of the rare small old bungalows remaining amid new, grandiose dwellings. When I arrived, there was a big commotion in front of his house. The street was blocked off by police cars and several fire engines. I found parking on a cross street and hurried over to the scene.

A crowd of neighbors and curious bystanders had gathered, and I squeezed my way through, only to be stopped by an official.

I said, "I have an appointment to see Dr. Unger."

"If you're talking about the man we found in the structure on fire, he's not going to see you anytime soon," he replied, pointing to a person on a stretcher who was being carried away by paramedics, loaded into the ambulance, and driven away, sirens blasting.

A hint of smoldering ash was still coming from the burnt down guesthouse behind the bungalow, but the firemen and firewomen seemed to have the blaze under control. I asked one of the onlookers what had happened and learned that there had been an explosion in the scientist's lab. And when I inquired whether the injured man had a family, the neighbor said, "Sure, he's got a wife and kid. The authorities are inside the house, trying to calm the woman down."

When the fire and police vehicles drove away, the group of curious neighbors slowly dispersed but not before voicing their concerns. I overheard someone say, "Having an experimental science lab in a residential area is too dangerous and should be against the law."

"I agree," said someone else. "We're lucky that the fire didn't spread. On a windy day, it could have easily jumped from roof to roof, endangering our entire neighborhood."

A third person commented, "I'm glad that it looks like it was only a chemical explosion. When I first heard and felt the big bang, I thought we were dealing with terrorists."

As the crowd dissolved, there was nothing left for me to do but also leave. Turning on the local news that evening, I heard that Jake Unger had suffered from third-degree burns all over his body and a fracture on his head, possibly caused by falling debris. He had died in the ambulance before it reached the emergency hospital.

CHAPTER 3

On impulse the next day, Sunday afternoon, I paid Jake Unger's widow a visit. I had slept poorly; the image of the stretcher with a wrapped-up body being carried away kept creeping into my mind. And I couldn't stop thinking about the wife and child I'd learned he had. I parked my Honda between a van and a BMW on the street in front of the Unger residence. As I rang the doorbell, it occurred to me that I might not be welcome.

The door was opened by a pretty young blonde with a male toddler in tow. She gave me a questioning stare.

"Mrs. Unger?" I asked.

She acknowledged the fact with a slight nod. I introduced myself and told her about my interview with her husband the previous day and my appointment to have a look at his laboratory, only to come upon the ghastly scene.

"Jake seems to have been popular yesterday," she said.

I didn't understand her comment but stored it away for later. Instead, I said, "I am so sorry for your loss. I came to see if I can be of help," and pointing to the vehicles parked at the curb, I added, "but you obviously have family and friends comforting you."

"No, there's no one here. The van belongs to the explosion investigators, who are in the backyard going through the rubble where the guesthouse used to be, and the other car most likely belongs to beachgoers."

She motioned me in, and as I followed her and the boy past the foyer to the living room, I was impressed by the young woman's ability to hide her sadness. As we sat down on her sofa, it became clear that she was more angry than grief-stricken.

She stated, "A good thing the firemen were here pronto, or the house would have gone up in smoke too. I told Jake weeks ago, when I smelled toxic chemicals coming from his lab, that he'll blow the place up one of these days."

"Do you have any idea what caused the explosion?"

She shrugged and said, "I leave that to the experts."

"The fire and explosion investigators only came today?"

"They were already here yesterday, examining the scene and collecting data, but came back again today."

The little boy had not made a sound so far but stayed close to his mom, and I wondered if he could talk. He seemed to take in our conversation with interest, though.

I said, "Mrs. Unger, I meant it when I offered my help, but I would like your assistance too. Like I mentioned when I introduced myself, I am a columnist and interested in your husband's discoveries concerning the contest he entered. As I understand it, he had invented - - or was close to inventing - - a fully biodegradable type of packaging."

"Call me Brenda, and my boy's name is Logan." She patted the toddler on the head and said, "He'll be three soon."

She continued, "As for Jake's discoveries, I have no idea what he was working on. He was involved in many projects and kept them all strictly secret, since he was paranoid that someone might steal his ideas. I didn't know he had entered a contest."

I tried not to show my surprise and changed the subject, inquiring about her folks, in-laws, and anyone else who would stand by her side in her time of need. I discovered that she had called her parents who lived out of state but had told them not to bother making the trip to California. Jake's mom and dad were both dead, and so far she had not called any of her friends.

I stated, "The explosion and what happened to your husband was mentioned on the local news station last night. No name was given, but people can put two and two together. You can't keep this a secret."

Then I said, "It may help to have your parents come."

"Why? There's nothing they can do."

"I was thinking of moral support."

"We're not that close."

Logan repeated, "Not that close," proving that he could indeed talk.

Brenda continued, "I did let Jake's brother know." And her anger flared up again as she went on, "The bastard had the nerve to tell me that I need to put the house up for sale now."

"I don't understand."

"Jake's parents owned this house and Jake inherited it. The will states that as long as he lives in it, the house is his, and if it is sold, both their sons will share the proceeds from the sale. Since I'm Jake's wife and Logan is his son, we own it now and have the right to live in it. There's nothing his scumbag brother can do about it." She paused and said, "Why on earth am I telling you all this?"

"Telling you all this," little Logan repeated.

His mom gave him a quick hug and then said, "Go play with your toys."

He obediently left us, and she called after him, "Don't take anything apart!"

To me she commented, "I'm afraid he takes after his father and has a scientific mind." That she was less than pleased about this was clear from the expression on her face.

I said, "He is way too young to understand what's happened and I hope that he won't miss his daddy for long."

"His daddy didn't find much time to spend with him anyhow, nor with me," she shot back. "He was devoted to science and nothing or nobody else."

I had obviously touched a sore spot and changed gears again, asking, "What did you mean when you said earlier that your husband seemed to have been popular yesterday?"

"Oh, it's just that lots of people besides you came to see him, which was unusual since he's basically a loner - - I mean, was."

"What kind of people?"

"There was his friend Julien. The top man at Astute came by. Jake's brother happened to be in Huntington Beach and showed up for a brief visit. Even a guy he hadn't seen in years dropped in, and God only knows who else. It was like Grand Central Station around here. I went to run errands and didn't come back until after the explosion. A good thing, too. Logan would have been traumatized had we both been here. A neighbor called 911 and the police and firemen beat me home."

"What's Astute?" I asked.

"It's an organization similar to the Mensa high IQ society, but its membership is limited to scientists."

"I take it that your husband was a member."

"Right, and he admired the organization's leader of the California chapter, coming close to worshipping him."

"But you don't?"

"I can't stand the guy."

Neither one of us talked for a few moments. I looked around the room, which was kept in perfect order and tastefully decorated with contemporary furniture. From where we sat on the sofa, we had a direct view to the big-screen TV. A few modern prints adorned the walls, but I did not see a single family photo anywhere. Baseball caps of different colors and logos stood like soldiers on the top of a china cabinet.

Pointing to them, I remarked, "Your husband was quite the collector."

She seemed embarrassed and said, "Oh, those are mine."

I heard Logan bang on what I presumed was a xylophone in the next room.

Brenda suddenly jumped up and said, "I didn't even offer you anything to drink. Sorry, but all I have is coffee, milk, or water."

"No thank you, I'm fine," I replied and she sat back down.

Another few seconds of silence went by, and then she said, "It really hasn't all sunk in, you know. I'm planning to call in sick at work tomorrow, and after dropping Logan off at preschool, I'll sort things out."

She looked extremely vulnerable at that moment, and I was trying to come up with something soothing to say. She didn't give me a chance, however, and burst out, "Oh crap! I have to make funeral arrangements."

"My offer to help stands. Do you want me to look into it?"

She stared at me for a second, seemingly undecided. Then she said firmly, "No. I have to do it myself. I owe him that much."

"Oh?"

"He paid for my education."

"Which is?"

With great pride, she stated, "I have a Bachelor of Science degree in dental hygiene from the West Coast University."

I tried to look duly impressed and got up to leave. Handing her my business card, I said, "If you change your mind or if you just want to talk, give me a call. Also, I'd be interested to know what caused the explosion."

On my short drive home I thought, I'll never hear from her; she doesn't *owe me* a thing. Her little boy may not be a talker and be reserved like his father, but he sure seemed to have grasped the gist of the conversation between his mom and me. And since I had a column due on Monday morning, I needed to set my mind to working mode.

CHAPTER 4

My job and private life kept me busy for the next few days. There was research and writing to be done, and I had interview appointments scheduled pertaining to an upcoming article about cruelty to animals. My personal habits consisted of working out at the gym Tuesdays and Thursdays and taking brisk walks on most other days. Sometimes on a whim, I would resort to riding my bicycle instead.

I had no social life to speak of; a couple of girlfriends that I occasionally saw movies or a show with was about the extent of it. My parents lived in Northern California. As their only child, I phoned Mom at least once a week. For company I had Midnight, my black cat.

As for men, I had given up on them for the time being. My last three relationships had not ended well, due to my knack for being attracted to the wrong kind. Number one kept a string of girlfriends beside me; number two turned out to be a drug addict; and the last one was a con-artist who swindled folks out of their hard-earned money. Since losers seemed to pull me like a magnet, it was best to abstain from further relationships.

To my surprise, Brenda Unger called and related the fire investigators' findings to me. She read from their report:

"Ammonium nitrate, which is a strong oxidizer, was identified as the cause of the explosion that set the structure on fire. Ammonium nitrate is combustible and explodes in the presence of heat. We discovered fragments of a heat lamp among the debris and determined that said heat lamp came into proximity of ammonium nitrate matter. Conclusion: The explosion was accidental due to careless handling of a flammable substance."

"So it was an accident," I commented.

"Of course! What did you expect?" Brenda replied, and I could tell that she was miffed. I thanked her for the information and we ended the call.

To be honest, until that very moment I had not suspected the explosion to be anything other than accidental. Now, as the words *careless handling of a flammable substance* registered in my mind, I started to have doubts. Would an esteemed scientist be that negligent? I asked myself. Moments later, I decided to put the suspicion out of my mind. Not my problem, I told myself. If the authorities determined the explosion was accidental and consequently closed the case, who was I to dispute it? Mind your own business and forget about it, I thought. And for a few weeks I was able to get by with that decision.

CHAPTER 5

Maybe I should devote a chapter to my neighbor, Mr. Apostolos, who lived in the apartment directly below mine. When I first moved in several years ago, he came to introduce himself and offer his help, if I ever needed it. Right off the bat, I decided to call him Mr. A - - Apostolos being a mouthful - - which was fine by him.

You guessed it, Mr. A was originally from Greece. He'd lived in the US for over 40 years, and his command of the English language was excellent, but a trace of an accent remained. He owned an antique shop in town, and although I was not particularly interested in antiques, I occasionally dropped by his store to be neighborly. On rare instances, I even made a purchase.

Now and then he presented me with small gifts - - a little personal trinket or a knick-knack, which I felt obligated to display in my apartment - - undoubtedly things he was unable to sell.

The trouble with Mr. A was that he liked to talk. That was certainly understandable. The man was in his sixties, had never been married, and had no family in the US. As far as I knew, he didn't have many friends. Mr. A divided his time between tending the antique store and accumulating new - - or I should say, old - - merchandise at auctions, flea markets, estate sales, and antique shows. The man was a dear but, as I already mentioned, lonely and chatty.

During the day he was elsewhere, but in the early mornings and evenings he was home as a rule. I tried to sneak by his apartment undetected when leaving or on my way in, avoiding him at his door where he tended to engage in endless conversation.

I felt bad about dodging him but had good reason. A few months earlier, he had asked me to write about his antique shop and treasures, as he called them, in one of my columns. I should have told him straight off that I wasn't the least bit interested in doing so. Instead, I had claimed to be too busy at the moment. Now he cornered me about it every chance he got.

Aside from all that, Mr. A was a convenient neighbor to have. He took care of Midnight when I was out of town, something I truly appreciated. Midnight even liked him, a fact that could not be taken for granted, as my big black cat didn't like just anybody. And most important, if I would ever be in any kind of trouble, I was positive that I could count on Mr. A for help.

CHAPTER 6

Now back to the main story. The contest was won by Dr. Julien Floyd, and a banquet was held in his honor on Saturday, May 26, at a luxury hotel in Irvine. I was still interested in the cause and arranged for admission to the event. I took my assigned seat at one of the tables in the large conference hall and observed the other guests. I presumed that besides the officers and employees of Tops & Associates, the room was filled with the winner's family, friends, fellow contestants, and prominent dignitaries in the field of science.

We were given a choice of red or white wine and an entrée of chicken or fish. I opted for Chardonnay and salmon. The man on my right introduced himself and stated his scientific credentials and then asked, "Are you by chance one of the contestants?" I told him my profession and that eco-friendly solutions were a concern of mine. He lost interest in me and turned to the person on his other side.

The ceremony began during dessert. The CEO of Tops & Associates gave a little speech, saying that soon all types of petroleum-based packaging would be obsolete. No longer would discarded bottles and containers litter our landscapes and oceans, but they would all be made from fully biodegradable cellulose-derived products. He took pride in his company that had instigated it all. Then he thanked the contestants for their submissions and stated that, while they all deserved merit, there was only one realistic and cost-efficient entry. And with great bravado he declared Dr. Julien Floyd the winner, asking him to come and get his reward. There was thunderous applause and cheering as the physicist made his way to the podium.

Once in the limelight, the CEO presented the doctor with a check and announced, "Here is your prize money of five million dollars!" And handing him another envelope, he commented, "Your hard work in the last year merits a vacation. Here is a two-week trip for two to Paris."

More clapping ensued. I looked around and noticed people's expressions. Most seemed genuinely happy for the winner, but some could not hide their disappointment. Probably fellow contestants, I thought.

Julien Floyd stepped up to the microphone and said, "I feel honored. Thank you so much!" Then he cleared his throat and stated, "The scientific community is a close-knit bunch and I know most of the contestants assembled here. They've all worked hard on this project and I almost feel guilty to be the chosen one." He held up his pointer and added with a smirk, "*Almost!*"

There was laughter in the room as he continued, "But let me get serious for a moment. I'm sure you've all heard about the tragic passing of my friend and colleague, Dr. Jake Unger. I happen to know that Jake was in the final stages of his own findings and would have contributed his version to the contest, had he survived. Please join me in a moment of silence for my friend."

One could have heard a pin drop in the next 20 seconds. When the moment passed, Julien Floyd stepped down from the podium and walked back to his table. The ceremony had come to a conclusion and some people left, while most still enjoyed their dessert and coffee. A small crowd stood in line to congratulate the proud winner. I waited until most had dispersed and then made my way over to him.

He had classic good looks with dark eyes and hair, and a strong Roman nose. He seemed more embarrassed than pleased with the congratulations people showered on him.

I said, "I'm the columnist Tara Blunt. You may not remember, but you refused to give me an interview a while back."

With a boyish grin he replied, "Oh, I do remember. Had I seen you in person, I'd have agreed to it, no doubt!"

Blatant flattery would normally not work for me, but I wanted to write a column about him and his discovery.

I said, "You see me now, Dr. Floyd, so let's do that interview soon."

"No problem. And please call me Julien."

I gave him a big smile and, handing over my business card, said, "Call me when you're ready, Julien."

CHAPTER 7

The call from Julien came two days later, and checking our calendars, we found we were both free for lunch on Wednesday, May 30. He suggested Ruby's at the end of the Huntington Beach pier. I parked the Honda half a mile away on a cross street, then walked down Main Street and onto the pier. I was early and first stopped to watch the volleyball players on the sand below. Of the dozen nets on both sides of the pier, a fourth were in use on that day. Then I walked on and about mid-pier stood still again to watch the surfers. It was one of those pleasant, sunny, spring days, with a temperature of 72 degrees and great waves for surfing.

I often came down to the ocean and the pier, yet each time the experience felt new to me. Looking down from my height of 100 feet above sea level, the young men and women appeared small on their boards, but I never grew tired of watching them.

I checked my watch. It was time to head toward the end of the long pier; so I followed other folks who walked in that direction. When almost at Ruby's, I heard someone close behind me say, "I finally caught you!" and turned my head.

A slightly out of breath Julien remarked, "You walk fast. I couldn't keep up, short of pushing people out of my way."

We were seated at a table by the window of the diner, giving us a view of nothing but ocean. I ordered a cheeseburger without bothering to look at the menu. Julien did likewise and had his with French fries, and I chose coleslaw as my side order. When served, we concentrated on eating.

Swallowing the last bite, and before I had a chance to start the interview, he said, "So you're a reporter."

"No, I'm a columnist."

"What's the difference?"

"A reporter is required to be unbiased in her reporting by stating the facts without voicing her own opinion. A columnist, on the other hand, may vent her own judgement freely."

He asked, "So how do you like your job?"

"I self-syndicate my column and am under freelancer contracts, which means I have to work hard but am basically my own boss. There are deadlines to be met, but I can arrange my workday according to my own schedule. As to whether I like it, my job can be challenging but also rewarding. And now, let's talk about you."

"Fair enough," he said.

I started with, "I googled you and learned that you have a PhD in physics and that you used to work for the government."

"No secrets are safe," he said with a smirk.

"So you studied quantum field theory, string theory, and so forth?"

"Mostly, 'and so forth,'" he replied, trying to keep cynicism out of his voice.

"I'm just curious, since you are basically a theoretical physicist, what got you interested in eco-friendly packaging?"

"For your information, I work on both theoretical and experimental projects. I admit, product packaging would not be my choice of study as a rule." He winked and said, "One has to make a living, and the prize money I've received is giving me a nice nest egg."

I inquired, "What are you planning to do with your five million?"

"After taxes, it will be considerably less," he replied. "But to answer your question, I'll spend a small amount of it on getting myself a proper lab. Right now, I work out of my apartment in Long Beach. With the rest, I'll finance my pet projects as I see fit."

"In other words, the money stays with science," I remarked.

"You bet!"

I suddenly thought of Jake Unger and compared the two scientists. The shy, introverted Jake, who had reminded me of a giraffe, and the cocky man sitting across from me. They were like day and night yet had the same calling.

I gathered a lot of data during the course of our lunch that day. Some of the information was later reflected in my column and some was off the record. I had brought a note pad along and jotted down the technical jargon and stored away the rest of his communication into my memory.

Julien shared that he had roomed with Jake and another man named Rob in an apartment in Arcadia, while the three had worked in a government-funded laboratory. A few years later, they had all gone their separate ways. He and Jake became self-employed, contracting with companies in the private sector, and Rob took a permanent job with a firm in Simi Valley.

I said, "And you all stayed friends?"

"Jake and I, yes. I occasionally get news from Rob, but the two of them no longer stayed in contact, as far as I know."

"How come?"

"They had a falling out over the quantum physics versus string theory buildup debate." He shrugged and added, "A bunch of nerdy physicists living under one roof was bound to cause friction. They hoped that the LHC experiments would prove one or the other wrong, but no such luck."

"What does LHC stand for?"

"Large Hadron Collider."

"The thing near Geneva, Switzerland?"

"Precisely that 'thing,'" he said, seemingly amused.

"On whose side of the argument are you?" I wanted to know.

"I keep an open mind."

We both looked out the window, watching a couple of seagulls fly by. When we focused on each other again, he asked, "Are you wearing colored contact lenses?"

"No. I have good vision."

"I could have sworn that your eyes were blue when we met at the ceremony and now they're definitely green."

"Oh, that. Someone once told me that they are translucent. Depending on the color of outfit I wear, they appear blue, gray, green, or gold. But let's not talk about my eyes."

I stated, "I interviewed Jake Unger on the morning of his death."

That threw him for a loop. He became quiet for several seconds. Then he asked, "What time was that?"

"Eight thirty. We met for coffee but he didn't tell me much."

"I'll be damned! I went to see him around ten o'clock and he didn't mention it. Frankly, I find it hard to believe that he gave you an interview."

I said, "Not only that, but I also had an appointment to get a look at his lab in the late afternoon."

"No way!" he burst out.

There was doubt in his expression as he made that outcry, and also something I could not put my finger on. Was it anger, mistrust, or fear?

Before I had time to sort it out, he explained, "Jake did not let people into his lab. He was paranoid that they'd steal his ideas. When I went to his guesthouse that morning, he closed the door to the lab, making sure we stayed in the other room."

I remarked, "In my case, he must have felt his work was safe, me being a layperson."

Then I decided to let him know that I was too late to see Jake's sanctum and related the scene to him that I found when I arrived at his colleague's address. He got somber as I talked, obviously grieving for his friend. I also told him about my visit to Brenda the next day, and her call to me later about the fire investigators' findings. Without going into details, I voiced my impression that Jake's wife was more angry than sad about his passing.

Julien nodded and said, "I can see her blaming him for blowing the place up. She has that kind of personality."

"So you know her well?"

"Not well but well enough. Jake should have never married her. She was too young for him and way too demanding. Come to think of it, he wasn't the marrying kind, period."

"What do you mean?"

"His sole passion was his work. He didn't have time for a wife and kid. You can't blame her for seeking happiness elsewhere." He covered his mouth and said, "Sorry! That slipped out."

I gave him an intent gaze and said, "Do you know this for a fact or are you guessing?"

"I know it firsthand. I saw her in action with her lover one day at - - -"

Holding up a hand, I said, "I don't need to know the particulars. I assume that you informed your friend about it."

"No, I didn't," he said. "There was no point in getting Jake upset. What he didn't know couldn't hurt him."

Before the interview came to an end I had one last question. I stated, "According to the fire investigators' report, the explosion was accidental due to careless handling of a flammable substance. Does that sound like your friend Dr. Jake Unger?"

"Not at all," he said, "Jake was extremely cautious. He must have been distracted."

I thanked him for his time, assuring him that only the professional and scientific facts pertaining to his winning

Tops & Associates' contest would be reflected in my column. Anything of a personal nature I would keep to myself.

As a rule, I picked up the check when interviewing people in a restaurant. Julien stopped me when I reached for my wallet and said, "You suppose I can afford to pay?"

CHAPTER 8

That evening, I worked on a rough draft of the information I had gathered from Julien's interview but had a hard time concentrating. It would have been nice to compare Jake Unger's discoveries to Julien's in my column, had I been in possession of the former's data. I remembered the interview with him at the Starbuck's clearly. He had been reluctant to say so, but I was under the impression that he had been ready to submit his project. And a few hours later, that project went up in smoke, never to reach the contest judges at Tops & Associates. I kept thinking that Jake might have shared his findings with me after his submission to the contest. Well, too late for me and certainly too late for him.

Thinking of Jake, I was finding it harder and harder to believe the accident was due to negligence on his part. According to his friend and colleague Julien, his wife, and what I had observed myself, the scientist had been careful and meticulous. So what was the alternative? That he was distracted like Julien had suggested? It was a possibility, but distracted by what? I asked myself. I thought that it was far more likely that someone had hit him over the head and then found a way to cause a chemical explosion.

With all the hazardous material abundant in a scientist's lab, that would have been an easy task.

I had no idea who would have been motivated to do so. After all, I did not know the man nor his circumstances, let alone his potential enemies. Why was I even racking my brain over this? I wondered. I told myself again, let it go! The authorities concluded that his death was accidental, so let it rest, Tara.

The draft of the column could no longer hold my attention. I chucked it for that night. Instead, I curled up with a book. In no time Midnight jumped into my lap, kneaded my thighs to find the perfect spot, and then settled down for a nap, purring at full volume.

Later in bed, instead of falling asleep right away, the conversation I had had with Brenda Unger entered my mind. She'd told me that lots of people had come to see her husband on the day of his death. The image of the pretty, young blonde emerged, with her angry expression as she stated, "It was like Grand Central Station around here."

Hell, I told myself, plenty of people had the opportunity to do away with him and his lab. Then I finally dozed off.

CHAPTER 9

On Friday, June 1, Julien phoned and I said, "If you want to know when the article about your project will appear in the paper, the answer is, not for another ten days. I have work that is scheduled first."

"Good to know but that's not why I'm calling. I noticed that there is no wedding ring on your finger, so I assume that you're not married. Are you seeing anyone?"

Oh no, he's going to ask me out, I thought, and replied, "No, and I want to keep it that way."

He said, "I was under the impression that we had a mutual attraction going on our lunch date the other day, but maybe I'm wrong."

"That was a business meeting not a date, and yes, you are wrong."

"How about meeting for coffee or something. I have an interesting proposition to make, which I'm sure you can't refuse."

I said, "I'm listening. You can tell me now."

"Okay, I will. As you've guessed, I'm also unattached." He paused, then continued, "There is nobody in my family or friends I care to share the trip I've won with. Will you join me for the two weeks in Paris?"

I was speechless.

"Are you there?" he asked.

"Sorry, I wasn't prepared for this."

I heard him chuckle, and he said, "I guess I sprung this on you without warning. You don't have to decide right now. The trip is good for any time I choose. Think on it."

I was staring at the phone long after we ended the call. Had I been honest when denying being attracted to him? There was chemistry between us, even if I refused to admit it. Yet, I had no interest in playing dating games, let alone a new relationship. I was still aching from the last one. And the notion that he wanted to spend his two weeks in Paris with *me*, a complete stranger, was laughable. He must have not been thinking clearly when he suggested it. He'll wake up tomorrow morning, scratching his head, wondering how he'd come up with such a crazy idea.

CHAPTER 10

A few days went by and the thought that it was possible someone had murdered Jake Unger, and got away with it, would not leave me alone. What to do? Going to the authorities was not an option. After all, my suspicion was nothing more than a gut feeling. Hire a private eye? Any self-respecting private investigator would laugh at me, suggesting that I come back when I had something concrete to offer. I decided it was up to me to do the detecting, even though I had zero experience in the field. Be creative, I told myself. And anyway, I was a columnist, digging for facts all the time. This was no different.

Since I needed lots more information from Brenda and possibly also from Julien, I had no choice but to let them know of my undertaking, fully realizing that both were potential suspects. Brenda was not thrilled when I indicated that we needed to talk once more, about an "important matter," was how I worded it.

She reluctantly agreed to see me in the early evening on June 5. When I arrived at her house, she was about to tuck Logan in. I didn't mind waiting.

Logan said, "Night, night," and the two vanished into the little boy's bedroom, leaving the door open. I listened as she read him a bedtime story, then sang a lullaby. I realized that, regardless of anything else, being a good mom seemed to be one of her traits.

Joining me in the living room minutes later, she said, "So what's the important thing you need to tell me?"

I asked, "Did it cross your mind that the explosion was not an accident?"

"Of course it was an accident; the fire investigators said so."

"They could be wrong."

She raised her voice. "What are you talking about? Are you suggesting Jake did it on purpose to kill himself?"

"No, that's not what I implied."

She stared. Then it appeared to dawn on her, and she said, "You've got some nerve, telling me that my husband was murdered."

"I'm not saying that he was, but I seriously think that it's a possibility."

"You're crazy!"

"How well did you know Jake?"

She gave me the evil eye and said, "What do you think! I lived with him for over four years."

"My point exactly." And I studied her for a second and then inquired, "May I ask how old you were when you got married?"

"I'm 23 now; you do the math."

At that moment I realized that Brenda had a sense of humor. I said, "Getting back to how well you knew your husband, would you say that he had a tendency to be negligent about his work?"

"Absolutely not. Even though I never understood his job, I know that he was meticulous in what he did. A couple of years ago, when he was under contract to work at a company's in-house laboratory, he wrote them a letter complaining about the safety standards at their lab."

We heard an outcry coming from Logan's room. Brenda got up and remarked, "He's having a nightmare. Let me check on him."

I heard her gently talking to her little boy in the next room, her words not much louder than a whisper, so that I couldn't make out what she said. Whatever it was seemed to soothe him, and he no longer made a sound. Again, it was clear to me that she had a flair for motherhood.

When she came back I said, "You read me the fire and explosion investigators' report over the phone, but may I have a look at it in person?"

"Sure, I'll get it," and with a shrug she went to fetch it, mumbling, "I can't see what's not clear about it."

I went over the investigators' findings carefully, reading the last sentence twice. The second time I read it aloud: "*The explosion was accidental due to careless handling of a flammable substance.*"

After some consideration, Brenda admitted, "You're right. Jake was never careless. I don't know why I didn't spot that myself." And seconds later she burst out, "But murder! I don't believe it. He could be annoying with his nit-picking, but that wouldn't be any reason to kill him."

"Can you think of any enemies he may have made?"

She shook her head.

"As you can imagine, I've given this some thought already. I'd like more information about the people who came by on the day of the explosion."

Her eyes widened as she exclaimed, "You think one of them - -"

She did not finish her sentence as the full implication sunk in.

I stated, "Somebody set something up in your guesthouse that day. Unless it was done by remote control - - which is unlikely - - people who came to see Jake are indicated."

Possibly she wanted justice for her husband, or else she realized that she herself could come under scrutiny. The result was that she cooperated. I learned that Jake's brother's name was Bryan and that he lived in Saugus. She volunteered his phone number. The top guy of Astute was Konrad König. She didn't have his number, but I was confident that it would be easy to find. The person whom Jake had not seen in years was a guy named Rob - - Brenda could not remember his last name.

When I told her that it would help if I knew the order in which people came by, she said that Julien Floyd was there in the morning and everyone else came in the afternoon, but that she didn't pay attention in what exact order.

I was reflecting on what other information I needed, when her smart phone buzzed. She pulled it out of her jeans pocket, looked at the text message, then answered with a short text of her own. As she focused her attention back on me, I said, "Just one more thing - -"

Her phone went off again and this time it rang. She glanced at the number, took the call and yelled, "Not now, dammit!" ended the call and clicked the phone off entirely.

So the young woman had a short fuse, I noted. She looked at me apologetically and I continued, "Was your guesthouse accessible through the inside of your home?"

"No, you had to go along the driveway on the outside. The guesthouse was in back, next to the garage. Now there's nothing left but the foundation."

"So you couldn't always know who came to the guesthouse, unless you happened to look out the window."

"True, but most people came here first and rang the doorbell. Jake doesn't - - I mean didn't - - like folks barging in on him unannounced."

I thanked her for her help and she saw me to the door.

As I pulled into my parking space at my apartment building, it occurred to me that the call might have come from Brenda's boyfriend, and she may have been terrified that he'd show up while I was there.

CHAPTER 11

If I pretended to be a private investigator, chances were slim that anyone would ask to see my credentials. In general, people tended to take others at face value. I wouldn't have to lie about it outright, just make sure that my targets would jump to that conclusion. I decided to try out my spiel on the victim's brother, Bryan Unger. I called him the next day and started to leave a voicemail message when he didn't answer, saying I was calling about his brother. He picked up as I was in mid-sentence. The following is the conversation we had:

"Am I speaking to Bryan Unger?"

"Yeah, who wants to know?"

"My name is Tara Blunt. I'm investigating the circumstances of Dr. Jake Unger's death and would like to interview you."

"What!"

I was starting to repeat myself when he interrupted. "I heard you the first time. What do you mean?"

"I can't go into details over the phone. I'm calling to schedule an appointment to talk with you in person."

"Are you with the police?"

"No, I'm private."

"What kind of investigating are you talking about?"

"Like I said, we can't do this over the phone."

"As far as I know, my brother died after an accidental explosion sent his laboratory up in smoke. Are you trying to tell me that the blast was deliberate?"

"I'm looking into that." And I said, "I know that you live in Saugus. I can interview you there whenever you like."

He grudgingly agreed to meet me on his day off, the following Monday afternoon, June 11, at the Saugus Café.

CHAPTER 12

My appointment with Bryan Unger was at two in the afternoon. I googled the directions and although the distance between Huntington Beach and Saugus was only 72 miles, allowing for moderate to sometimes heavy traffic, the estimated driving time was a few minutes short of two hours. I ate an early lunch and then headed out the door at noon for my drive north, first on the I-405 and then the I-5 freeways.

I had looked up the Saugus Café and discovered that it was an old-school diner, established in 1887. It was listed as among the oldest restaurants in Los Angeles County. In its heyday, the place had often been patronized by celebrities.

I arrived a few minutes early. Most of the lunch crowd was leaving or had already gone. As soon as I sat down in one of the booths, the friendly waitress handed me a menu. I wasn't hungry but was curious. The breakfast choices were substantial. For lunch there was a huge selection of burgers, sandwiches and salads; and they offered a great variety of classic entrees for dinner. Although the food was nostalgic, it was the atmosphere of the place that captured my interest, with the Jukebox blaring oldies and the waitresses calling locals by their names.

I had a clear view of the entrance from where I sat so I saw Bryan Unger come in. He was tall like his brother had been and they resembled each other physically, but that was the extent of their similarity. Whereas the scientist had been reserved and tongue-tied, it soon became clear that Bryan was a talker.

I got up and waved him over. When we stood eye to eye I said, "Mr. Unger? I'm Tara Blunt," and gave him a firm handshake. Then I motioned him to the vinyl seat across the table from mine, and as we both sat down, he uttered in disbelief, "*You*'re a private investigator?"

"What did you expect?"

"Someone older, tougher, and uglier."

I judged him to be still in his twenties, so I commented, "I'm way older than you and stronger than I look. As for the rest, thank you!"

"Do you carry a gun?"

The question caught me off guard, realizing that I hadn't thought my role all the way through. I recovered fast and replied, "Not right now. Should I be worried?"

"Not on my account," he said, lifting both arms up above his head in a mock surrender gesture.

I stated, "Enough about me. First off, I'd like to declare that I am sorry for your loss."

He bowed his head. I couldn't tell whether in acknowledgement or out of embarrassment.

The pleasant waitress came and took our orders. We both had eaten lunch, so we ordered apple pie and coffee.

I continued, "As I told you over the phone, I'm looking into your brother's death."

"You suspect there was foul play?"

"I cannot give out that information while the investigation is ongoing."

He said, "Well, it's obvious that you do. Nobody from the police contacted me."

"That may soon change," I said with a meaningful glance. "Let me ask you a few questions concerning you and your brother. Were you his only sibling or are there others?"

"No, it was just Jake and me."

I almost gave myself away by telling him that I'd met Dr. Unger on the morning of his death and then caught myself, changing the wording of my question to, "I understand that there was quite an age difference between you and your brother."

"Yes, Jake was ten years older. Our parents added me as an afterthought."

"May I ask what you do for a living?"

"I work in sales at a car dealership." With a begrudging grin he added, "We can't all be geniuses like Jake was."

"So he was pretty special growing up?"

"He was a brain, and I admit, I was the black sheep."

"Oh?"

He shared, "I realized early on that I could never measure up, so I stopped trying. In high school, I got involved with the wrong crowd of friends and messed up mega time, but I won't go into all that. I ended up not going to college, which pissed my folks off. But then, I wasn't their favorite son to begin with, so no big harm done."

He looked away from me, appearing to be deep in thought, and added, "I've cleaned up my act since then and am successful in my own way. Too bad my parents didn't live long enough to know it."

We were served, and for a short time we both concentrated on eating our delicious pies.

Then Bryan remarked out of the blue, "In the 1930's, stars like Clark Gable, Gary Cooper, and John Wayne may have been sitting in our booth, enjoying a quiet meal away from the Hollywood crowd."

"No wonder the place got me nostalgic on first sight," I said, "but let's get back to business. I talked to your brother's widow and found out that there's a dispute between you and her about the house in Huntington Beach."

I took a notebook out of my large bag, glanced at my scribbles, and continued, "According to her, Dr. Unger inherited your parents' home under the condition that he and his family live in it. If sold, however, the proceeds from the sale would go to both their sons. She is under the impression that, as Dr. Unger's widow and son, she and little Logan legally own the house. She also informed me that you are pressuring her to sell the property."

It was obvious that he became furious during my little speech. He burst out, "Leave it to Brenda to twist everything in her favor, the bitch!"

"Tell me your version, then, Mr. Unger."

"Call me Bryan, and stop calling my brother Dr. Unger, for crying out loud! A simple Jake will do."

"Noted."

He said, "Here is the deal: It is true that the house belonged to Jake. Let me backtrack. Years ago, our parents moved to Florida but kept their house in Huntington Beach. Jake was single then and rented the place from them, as he had quit his government job and became self-employed. Then Mom and Dad both got killed in a horrible car crash."

"I'm so sorry," I interrupted.

"Anyhow, they had made a will and in it was the clause that Jake would inherit the house as long as he lived in it. Also stipulated was that if we lived in it together, it would belong to both of us. Not that I'd have been interested in rooming with Jake. And as you stated correctly, if the house were sold, the proceeds would be divided equally between Jake and me. Mind you, Jake was still single at the time of my parents' passing. He married Brenda about a year later."

He looked me in the eye and said, "So you see, now that Jake is gone, Brenda has no claim to the place."

I inquired, "Would you want to live in it?"

"No, but that's not the point. I have a right to demand that it is sold." He shook a fist up in the air and declared, "I'm looking into hiring a lawyer. Brenda can't get away with keeping what is rightfully mine."

"Good luck with that. Now back to my investigation. I understand that you paid Jake a visit on the day of his death. What was the occasion?"

He grinned and said, "You're well informed. I bet that blabbermouth Brenda told you. It so happened that I took my girlfriend to the annual Taste of Huntington Beach event, where we enjoyed many delicious tastes from local restaurants and sips from top wineries. I couldn't be in Surf City without saying hello to Jake, now could I?"

"I guess not. Did your girlfriend accompany you when visiting your brother?"

"No, she wasn't exactly a fan of Jake's and didn't feel like coming along, preferring to stay at a bar on Main Street."

"At what time did you get to your brother's place?"

"Sometime in the afternoon; I didn't look at my watch." And the implication suddenly seemed to occur to him. He stared at me and then blurted, "You don't think I had anything to do with the explosion?"

"At this stage of the game, I keep an open mind," I said.

From that point on, Bryan was no longer Mr. Talkative. Either afraid that he had said too much, or perhaps miffed that I considered him one of the suspects, he promptly clammed up. No matter, the interview was coming to an end, regardless. I thanked him for coming, picked up the check, and left.

On the long drive home I rehashed our talk. It was evident that no love had been lost between the two brothers. Did Bryan resent his older, brainy sibling enough to deliberately blow him and his lab to pieces? During the conversation with Brenda I had gleaned that she hated her brother-in-law. Now it was obvious that he returned her sentiment. Whether or not Bryan Unger was my culprit, I understood his eagerness to sell the house. Although the small old bungalow was not impressive, the location where it stood was. Property that close to the ocean would easily fetch a million and a half. Whether he had the legal right to sell it was another matter.

CHAPTER 13

Although I didn't like the idea of taking Julien into my confidence, I figured that I had no other choice. He answered my call on the second ring when I phoned that same evening. Before I had a chance to inform him of my venture he said, "So you've decided to accept my offer?"

My mind was in detective mode, and except for my job, I had managed to erase everything else from my brain. I almost asked, "What offer?" before I grasped that he was talking about the Paris trip.

"I'm still indecisive, but I'm calling about something else entirely," I replied. And I told him about my suspicion and then gave him a short version of the discussions I had had with Brenda and Bryan.

He heard me out. Then he said, "Even if you're right, and I'm not saying that you are, why not leave the detective work to the professionals?"

I stated, "The authorities concluded that the explosion was accidental and as far as they're concerned, the case is closed. So far, I have no evidence to prove them wrong, and I can't go to them until I do."

He chuckled and said, "So you're impersonating a private investigator, that's funny."

"Don't patronize me."

"I'm sorry. I didn't mean it in a condescending way." He paused and then commented, "You seemed to have fooled Bryan, so it's possible that your scam might work with others too."

I put in, "I don't consider it a scam. I may not be licensed, but I am investigating Jake Unger's death."

"Fair enough. You are obviously seeking my assistance. How can I help?"

A beep told me that I had another caller on the line. I recognized the number and told him, "I have to put you on hold for a sec."

I switched over. "Hi, Mom. I'm talking to someone else. Call you right back."

Returning to Julien I said, "Sorry! Where were we?"

"I was offering my help."

"Right, and I need it. Brenda told me that somebody whom her husband had not seen in years came by on his fateful last day. The person's first name was Rob, but she couldn't remember his last name. I presume it's the same Rob you told me about who roomed with you and Jake many years ago."

"Rob's last name is Cloud. What a coincidence that he chose that day to get back in touch with Jake." There was a pause in the line, then he added, "Unless it wasn't a coincidence."

"I'm determined to find out," I said. "Do you have his number?"

Julien not only gave me the number but the address too. He was a source of information on another matter as well. It so happened that he was also a member of Astute and had the number of the organization's top guy in California handy, a man named Konrad König. He was equally surprised that König had paid Jake a visit and stated that he didn't think the man normally made house calls. And Julien also informed me that König had been present at the banquet ceremony where Tops & Associates had handed over the prize money.

Then I said, "Brenda mentioned that there had been an unusual amount of people who came to see her husband that day. I'm curious, why did you drop in on your friend that morning?"

He laughed and asked, "So I'm a suspect too?"

"Of course. Everyone concerned is," I replied.

He mocked me, "Of course!" Then he got serious and said, "For the record, I was ready to submit my findings to Tops & Associates and on a whim decided to check with Jake about how he was coming along and compare notes. He was having none of it. As a matter of fact, he got angry and thought that I was out to spy on him. That was ridiculous, since I had my solution and was ready to submit my data, including a prototype."

Then he said, "I can understand that you are gung-ho on detecting but keep in mind that the explosion may have been an accident, pure and simple. Jake may have been absent-minded and placed the ammonium nitrate too close to the heat lamp."

"Maybe."

Before we ended the call he said, "By the way, I saw your column in today's paper. It reads well and you got all the technical terminology correct. Thanks for the nice things you wrote about me and my discovery!"

"I meant every word," I said.

CHAPTER 14

Midnight and I were enjoying the end of the evening stretched out in front of the TV when Mom called again.

"What *is* going on?" she demanded to know. "First you don't call all week, and when I phone and find you busy talking with someone else, you don't get back to me."

"So sorry, Mom, I completely forgot."

"That's obvious. So what gives?"

I was not about to tell her about my venture and said, "There's nothing going on, I've been extremely busy with work lately. That's all."

"Well, there's plenty going on here. Your dad is having a mid-life crisis."

"At 59? You're kidding?"

"I know it's absurd. It was bad enough when he went to a rap and hip-hop performance, but now he's going to purchase a motorcycle. He's going to get himself killed! Perhaps you can talk some sense into him. I'll put you on speaker."

Dad came on the line and said, "Hello Tara. Don't listen to your mom, she's making a big deal out of nothing."

"What kind of bike do you have in mind, something like a scooter?"

"Don't be silly, that would be just a step up from a bicycle. I saw a hog advertised that I'm interested in; it's a beauty all right."

Mom interrupted, "Next thing we'll know is that he joined a motorcycle gang!"

I ignored her and said, "So Dad, where are you planning to ride?"

"On the road, certainly not in our back yard. Are you high on something? Now that they've legalized pot in California, I wouldn't be surprised."

"No, I'm not into marijuana, but don't change the subject. What I meant is, are you planning to ride on the freeways or only on local streets around your neighborhood?"

"Wherever the whim takes me; that's the beauty of it. I'll be free to roam around the country."

Oh boy, I thought, he's really going through a mid-life crisis, and what's more, he's got it badly.

Into the phone I said, "You haven't bought it yet, right?"

"I'll head over to the Harley-Davidson dealer tomorrow."

"Do us all a favor, Dad. Think it through some more before you do."

He didn't answer but asked instead, "So what's happening with you? Are you dating again?"

"No."

"Don't wait too long; you're not getting any younger."

Mom said, "Don't pester her. She'll see men again when she's good and ready."

I didn't have the heart to tell them that I may never "see men again" ever.

CHAPTER 15

The following day was a Tuesday, so I went to the gym for my exercise routines early in the morning. I started off with a ten-minute Pilates workout. Next, I went over to the equipment area. There was a fair crowd of people eager to exercise before starting their workdays. No one was using the large, intimidating cable pulley machine located smack in the middle of the gym. I headed straight for it. By doing different moves, the cable pulley targeted the abs and also toned the arms and legs.

To continue my routine, I found an unoccupied treadmill and stepped onto it. I started with a comfortable walking pace, then upped the speed to a faster stride, accelerating it to a jog, and finally to a running tempo. I held the run for five minutes, until I could feel my heart beat rapidly. Then I switched back to a lesser pace, finishing the workout with a cool-down walk.

I was sitting on a bench in the hallway with a towel over my head, debating if I should call it quits for the day and hit the shower or have another go at the cable pulley machine. From a bench on the opposite side of the hallway, I heard a man say, "Stay put and wait for me. I need to assist someone with weight training for a few minutes, then I'm free for the next couple hours."

A woman answered, "I can't. I need to get my boy from the kiddy gym class, drop him off at preschool, and then get to work."

I knew that voice! I peeked from behind my towel. Sure enough, Brenda Unger sat there in conversation with a man I had seen around the gym many times. I did not know his name but assumed that he worked there as an instructor and trainer. Neither one of them paid me any attention. Still, I realized it was best if I kept a low profile, so I left the hand towel in place.

They kept their voices low, and I strained to overhear the rest of their talk.

He said, "I'll come see you tonight, then."

"No. You'd better not," she replied.

"Why are you avoiding me lately?"

Brenda stated, "We have to be careful. It may be best if we cool it for a while."

"What do you mean? The exact opposite is the case. The way things have turned out, we no longer have to sneak and hide!"

"People may get the wrong idea."

"What people? And what the hell are you talking about?"

"Someone's looking into things."

"What kind of things?"

"The explosion," she said. "Anyhow, I need to go. I'll call you later."

I lowered the towel in time to see her walk away. The trainer called after her, "Wait!" but she didn't turn around.

Shaking his head, he got up too and then marched in the direction of the weight room.

I stayed seated on the bench a few moments longer, thinking about what I had overheard. Julien was spot on with his claim that Brenda had a boyfriend. And what was more, she worried about me finding out about it. Interesting!

Then I headed toward the showers at long last.

CHAPTER 16

As I mentioned at the beginning, I am not a seasoned book author and my lack of structural finesse may show, but it is at this point of the story that the detective work got interesting, and I was becoming exceedingly intrigued. First though, I experienced an episode of a personal matter.

On Thursday of that week, I came back from the supermarket in the early evening carrying a grocery bag in each hand. I was fumbling for my keys to the apartment when the door was opened from the inside.

I nearly dropped my groceries and cried out, "Dad! Are you trying to give me a heart attack?"

He ignored my remark, gave me a hug, and said, "About time you showed up. Your cat is making a racket. Do you ever feed him?"

"Dad, I gave you a key to my apartment in case of an emergency, but you scared me half to death. Why didn't you call first? And where is Mom?"

I stepped past him, and he followed me into the kitchen. I grabbed a can of cat food from one of the bags, and while I pacified Midnight, Dad answered, "She's home. I didn't invite her along; she'd be scared to ride anyway."

"Oh no! Is that your motorcycle parked up front?"

"Yep. That's my hog. Isn't it a beauty?"

"You didn't waste any time!"

He grinned and said, "Nope. Bought it Tuesday and was on my way yesterday. Say, may I spend the night on your couch? I'm only passing through, but might as well save me the hotel bill."

"No problem. I'm planning to fix spaghetti and Italian sausage for dinner. You're welcome to join me."

"Sounds good. Thanks, Tara." And he chuckled and said, "You have a protective neighbor living on the floor below. He almost called the police on me."

"What did you do to Mr. A?"

"That's a name?"

"No, I just call him that, but hurry up and tell me what happened."

Dad said, "He followed me up the stairs and when I put the key in your lock, he yelled, 'Hold it right there or I'll call the cops!' And then he didn't take my word for it that I'm your dad. I had to show I.D. to convince him that our last names were the same. And once he realized that I was legit, I couldn't shut him up. Among other stuff, he said that he'd seen me park the Harley from his window, and when he realized I was getting into the apartment building and then heard me walking past his door, he got suspicious. Your Mr. A apparently noticed when coming home minutes earlier, that your car was not parked in its spot."

"Good to know he has my back," I remarked.

I unpacked the rest of the groceries and then set out to prepare the meal. To my surprise, Dad washed the lettuce and tomatoes and then tossed the salad. As far as I could remember, he had never helped Mom in the kitchen. Dad was full of surprises these days.

I'm not the best cook, but he seemed to enjoy the meal and even went for seconds. After all, it's not easy to ruin spaghetti and sauce.

I waited until our plates were empty before bringing up the subject, asking, "So what's going on with you?"

"Nothing wrong with enjoying life for a change," he shot back.

"Are you keeping Mom posted about your traveling plans?"

"I can't tell her where I'm going when I don't know it myself."

"But you're calling or texting along the way, right?"

"I left my phone at home."

"You're kidding! You forgot your smartphone?"

He stated, "No, I didn't forget; I left it behind on purpose and feel free as a bird."

I got up and cleared away the dishes, thinking, he's got it worse than I thought. I didn't dare imagine how frantic Mom must be. Taking off on a motorcycle was one thing, but shedding all responsibilities was another. I wished there was something I could say to make him come to his senses but knew him well enough to realize that any argument was useless. His so-called mid-life crisis needed to run its course.

Coming back to the table, I asked, "How long a trip are you planning?"

"Three weeks or a month."

"What if something happens to Oma?"

"Something already happened to her, and if she should pass away, it would be a blessing for all concerned."

"I was thinking of Mom," I said, pointing out, "She would have to drive down on her own and take care of things."

He shrugged his shoulders and said, "Don't be such a worrywart."

"And your job?"

"What about it?"

"Don't tell me you quit?"

"I haven't taken a proper vacation in years. They owe me at least a month," he stated.

"You cleared it with your boss, though?"

"Yep. Told him I'm taking to the road in my Harley for a while." He grinned. "You should have seen his face: green with envy."

"I always thought that being an engineer suited you and that you liked your job."

"I thought so too. Now I'm sick of the same routine: getting up at the *same* time every morning, eating the *same* boring breakfast, then fighting the freeway only to sit down at the *same* desk, doing the *same* boring job, day after day, year after year."

"I get it, Dad! So you need a change from your routine, bought a motorcycle and hit the road. Could this have anything to do with the fact that you'll turn 60 in a couple of months?"

"Not a darn thing."

"But you must have a general idea where you're going," I insisted.

"So far, I came down the coast and had a blast on some of the curvy stretches along Highway 1. Tomorrow, I'll head inland, maybe take Interstate 10, going south. On it, I could ride through Arizona, New Mexico, Texas, and Louisiana. Heck, I could end up at the French Quarter in New Orleans."

"So that's your plan? You'll ride all the way to New Orleans on Interstate 10?"

"Perhaps."

He changed the subject and, looking at me sideways, asked, "Have I ever told you that I'm proud of you?"

"All the time while growing up."

"I meant as an adult."

"Probably. I can't remember," I said, wondering where he was going with that.

"Well, I am. You've accomplished a lot and continue to make a name for yourself as a columnist, but all work and no play is not a good idea. You need to have a balance."

I opened my mouth and was about to assure him that I had plenty of balance, when he held up his hand to stop me, seeming to know what I meant to express.

He said, "You keep in shape by going to the gym, et cetera, but there's more to life than that. You're young and need to have some fun. Go out dancing to clubs and meet people."

I laughed and said, "The other day on the phone you told me that I was getting old, practically accused me of 'being over the hill,' and now you're telling me I should behave like a college kid!"

"Exactly my point. Get out there and mingle."

"What you really mean, Dad, is that you want me to go out and find a man. Sorry to disappoint, but I'm not in the mood."

"Don't wait too long. You don't have any siblings," - - I did not say it aloud but thought, and whose fault is that? - - as he continued, "so you're the only hope for your mom and me to ever have grandchildren."

Midnight jumped onto my lap. While petting him, I said, "Let me call Mom and tell her you're with me."

"She'll want to talk to me and I don't feel like listening to her cry. You can call her tomorrow, if you like."

Nothing more was said about Dad's adventure nor my needing to go out and meet people. We watched a bit of TV, and then I made the couch ready for him with a pillow and a blanket. I did not hear him leave, but when I woke up early the next morning, he was gone.

CHAPTER 17

"All the way to New Orleans!" Mom shouted into the phone. "What's he planning to do when he gets there?"

"Live it up at the French Quarter is my guess."

She yelled, "The shameless wanderer!"

"Just kidding. I'm not even sure it's where he'll end up. He was vague about it. And anyhow, he might change his mind about where he's going a hundred times, for all we know," I assured her.

"What am I supposed to do? Twiddle my thumbs until he feels good and ready to come home? I haven't slept a wink since he left and I bet he slept like a baby on your couch."

I could tell she was crying as she continued, "When he refused to take his phone along and I argued that I wouldn't even know whether he's okay or not, he had the audacity to say that since he was equipped with a driver's license, the police would contact me in case of an accident. Can you believe it?"

"Yes, that sounds like Dad."

Her misery gave way to anger as she cried out, "His behavior is totally reckless, befitting a teenager, not a man approaching 60! One of the reasons I was initially attracted to your dad and what kept me admiring him all these years, was his logical mind and sense of responsibility. Now he's unreasonable and has lost all perception of obligation." And she added, "I'm afraid he's losing his mind as well."

"You're exaggerating," I said.

"Oh yeah? You think his conduct is normal?"

"I admit, he's going through something right now. But Mom, it's not the end of the world. He needs some space and time alone. You were right, he's in a mid-life crisis, but it could be worse. Some men have affairs when they go through it."

"What about me?" she yelled. "Am I permitted a crisis?"

"I don't see why not," I humored her.

"All right then, I'll have an affair."

"Good for you!" I exclaimed and heard her forced laughter.

After we hung up, I thought, she couldn't have been serious, or was she?

CHAPTER 18

Friday and Saturday I was busy doing research for my columns, but for Sunday, June 17, I scheduled an interview with Rob Cloud in Simi Valley. I had googled him beforehand and learned that he had a doctorate in science. I was getting to know a lot of doctors these days. At his suggestion, we met in a public park and settled on a bench at the picnic area. There was not a hint of June gloom, and people enjoyed a stroll through the park in the late afternoon, but the place was far from being crowded. Faint noises reached us from the kids' playground nearby, yet we had plenty of privacy to talk undisturbed.

Rob Cloud had taken my statement over the phone of an ongoing investigation into the explosion at Jake Unger's place at face value and seemed to assume that I was a private investigator. I had also explained that I was interviewing everyone who came to see Dr. Unger on that fateful day. When I met the man in person, I found him a bit pathetic. His head was shaved on the sides and down the back, but what remained of his hair was held together in a tiny ponytail, sticking straight up at the crown. The hairstyle would have suited a high school or college student but looked ridiculous on a man in his late thirties.

He may have been a brainy scientist, but it soon became obvious that Rob was socially awkward.

I extended my hand in greeting and said, "Hello, Dr. Cloud. What a great idea to have our talk in the park on such a lovely day."

He ignored my hand and remarked, "My shrink said I need to get out more often."

I didn't know how to respond to that, and he continued, "He wants me to meet people, especially women. Are you single?"

I realized that I needed to be direct with this man and said, "That's irrelevant. As you well know, this meeting is strictly business."

He jumped right to the crux of the matter and said, "I'm sorry about Jake," and seemed sincere.

"What do you know about what happened?"

"He was killed in an explosion in his lab."

"What is your theory about that?" I asked.

"I don't have any. You tell me."

"As mentioned over the phone, I'm looking into it, but I'd like your opinion."

"I don't know anything," he said, "other than what I read in the paper and heard on the news."

A ball came flying. I caught it and threw it to the kid who came chasing after it. Then I turned back to my suspect and asked, "Did you by chance enter the contest sponsored by Tops & Associates regarding eco-friendly packaging?"

"Oh, you know about the contest. I'd have liked to participate but couldn't. My time is limited and belongs to my employer. It would have caused a conflict. All my discoveries are the property of the company I work for."

"I see."

"Actually, a former roommate of mine won the contest."

"Yes, Dr. Julien Floyd," I stated.

His grey eyes widened as he said, "You know a lot!"

"I made it my business to know everything and everyone remotely connected to the late Dr. Unger. Speaking of which, what did you think of him?"

He stared and said, "I don't follow."

"I'm aware that besides Dr. Floyd, you also roomed with Dr. Unger. So you must have formed an opinion of him."

Without hesitation he declared, "Jake was a brilliant physicist, simply brilliant. I haven't met anyone who comes close to his genius."

"But?"

"The man was stubborn as a mule."

I inquired, "Why did you drop by his place on Saturday afternoon, April 14, on the day of his death?"

He was close to pouting and said, "I just paid him a friendly visit, is all."

"From what I heard, you and Jake Unger weren't on friendly terms."

He was not pleased that I was so well informed. After an entire minute of silence, while pulling nervously at his tiny ponytail, he said, "It was time to bury the hatchet."

"Because?"

There was another pause. Then he divulged, "I needed a favor. Like I said, my shrink wants me to become more social. I figured that I might as well start with becoming a member of Astute." He pulled at his ponytail again and explained, "That's a high IQ society for scientists."

"I've heard of Astute," I commented.

"Anyhow, one needs a recommendation to join. I knew that Jake was a member and that he and Konrad König, the leader of the California chapter, were buddies. I admit that I crawled back to Jake that day because I needed him to put in a good word for me with König."

"Did he?"

He looked at me like I was an idiot and said, "He hardly got the chance!"

"I meant, did Dr. Unger promise that he would?"

"Not exactly. Jake never talked much, but I think he was going to."

I could not let on that I had met Jake Unger, but Rob was right: His fellow scientist had been a man of few words.

I inquired, "At what time did you get to his place and how long did you stay?"

"It was in the afternoon. I don't remember the time and I wasn't there long. Ten or fifteen minutes, max. I was under the impression that he wanted me to leave. He kept looking at the time."

"Did you meet in the house or at his lab?"

"I rang the doorbell of the main house. His wife answered it, telling me that he was working in the lab, and directed me to the guesthouse out back."

"Was he working on an interesting project?"

He replied, "I have no idea. He shut the door to the lab and we stayed in the other room."

I asked, "Did you part as friends?"

"Yes, we made peace."

There was nothing else I could think to ask, so I ended the interview.

He got up and, pointing at the top of his head, said, "This is part of the new social me. How do you like it?"

"It makes a statement," I replied.

Then we said our good-byes. Again, he avoided shaking hands. I sat on the picnic bench a tad longer, watching him walk away, his little ponytail sticking up like a waterspout. Even his gait looked awkward.

I had plenty of food for thought on the long drive home from Simi Valley. It was time to take Konrad König under scrutiny. I hoped that he did not remember seeing me at that banquet event held in Julien's honor. Chances were slim that he would, with hundreds of people attending, but it was possible.

CHAPTER 19

The phone call to Konrad König did not go well. I introduced myself and the dialogue went something like this:

"Sarah who?"

"It's Tara with a 'T' and the last name is Blunt, like a blunt instrument."

He barked, "Never heard of you."

"I'm looking into the cause of the explosion on April 14 at Dr. Unger's guesthouse."

"What has that got to do with me?"

"I assume you're aware that Dr. Unger died as a result of that explosion," I said.

"Absolutely. I attended his funeral."

"Well, sir, I'm interviewing everyone concerned, especially people who paid him a visit on that day."

"I can't help you."

"All the same, I'd appreciate a talk face to face."

"My time is limited, and like I said, I can't help you," he repeated.

"I understand that you're a busy man and guarantee that this won't take long. You pick the day and time."

"You sure are an obstinate woman!"

There was a long silence. I imagined that the wheels in his head were turning. If he refused to see me, I might think he had something to hide. On the other hand, we both knew that I could not force him into giving me an interview.

I thought that he had hung up when he snapped, "Fifteen minutes this Thursday the 21st at 5:00 p.m.," and he gave me the address of Astute headquarters in Orange County. With a name like Konrad König, I had expected a German accent but there had not been a trace. The man was obviously US born.

CHAPTER 20

I arrived three minutes early. There were only a few vehicles parked in the big parking lot of the Astute building, so I had my pick and waited in the car. At five o'clock sharp, I opened the door to the main entrance and found myself in a small reception area, similar to a physician's waiting room.

"I'm Tara Blunt to see Konrad König," I told the young woman sitting behind the counter.

"He's expecting you," she said, and I followed her down a hallway with what I assumed were office rooms to each side. At the end of the passage, she led me through a hall as large as a ballroom. Floor-to-ceiling bookcases stood along the parallel walls and a gigantic whiteboard at its head. Folding chairs were stacked up high at a corner area. The receptionist marched me through the vast space, our pumps echoing with rhythmic tapping along the empty hall. When we arrived at a side door, she held it open for me and retreated, saying, "Go on in."

A second later, I stood in front of the "king" himself, seated at the desk in his sanctum. He got up to acknowledge me, and shaking hands, I asked, "Is it *Dr.* König?"

"I have a doctorate in physics and teach it at a major university, if that's what you want to know," he said and looked at his watch, making it clear that he was timing my fifteen minutes.

He was in his fifties, a big man of about 6'3" and maybe 230 pounds, with an ego to match. I did not remember seeing him at the ceremony held in Julien's honor, but to my dismay he said, "You look familiar. Have we met before?"

"Not to my knowledge," I replied, and quickly added, "I'm aware that your time is limited, but please give me an idea what Astute is all about."

"It's a high IQ society. Our non-profit organization is a forum of intellectual exchange among members. The purpose is to nurture human intelligence and provide an inspiring scientific environment through lectures, discussions, and journals. We even offer research assistance. There are professional and social gatherings, and we publish magazines and newsletters with articles written by members."

"I take it that it's not easy to join your organization."

He stated, "To become a member, first and foremost, one has to be a scientist, and I don't accept anyone with an IQ below 130. A recommendation from an existing member also helps."

"Now to get to the reason for our talk. I understand that you knew Dr. Unger well," I said.

Instead of answering he probed, "Who hired you?"

I was ready for that question and surprised that he was the first of my suspects to ask it. I replied, "I'm not at liberty to say. Now then, Professor König, why did you pay Dr. Unger a visit on the day of his death?"

"Jake asked me to come by."

"For what reason?"

"That's confidential."

I stated, "Under the circumstances, I need to know, so I advise you to tell the truth."

He gave me a venomous stare and said, "My seeing Jake on that day had nothing to do with his death and is none of your business."

"Since we're dealing with a potential homicide, I'm making it my business."

"As far as I know, the chemical explosion was a tragic accident."

I did not comment, just looked him in the eye and waited.

He said, "Our society lost a physicist of the highest caliber, and I lost a friend in Jake. He was a quiet, unassuming fellow. The idea that someone murdered him is absurd."

I held his gaze and waited some more.

Seconds later, König finally gave in and told the reason why Jake Unger had asked him to come by that day. I learned that Jake had informed him that he had made a beneficiary change to his life insurance policy. Years ago, after the fatal accident of his parents, Jake had gone through a period of self-doubt and also showed concern about his own mortality. König, as his mentor, gave him moral support during that difficult time. In return, Jake had taken out a life insurance policy, insisting on making his mentor the beneficiary. This was before his marriage to Brenda.

On that lethal Saturday in April, Jake had been apologetic, telling König that he was changing the insurance policy's beneficiary in favor of his wife. Apparently, Brenda had pressured him ages ago to do so. He had told her that he'd make the change but forgot all about it and was doing so just then.

"Interesting," I remarked.

He stated, "I told him that I was cool with that. Making me the beneficiary had been done on a whim on his part to begin with. That his wife and child would become the recipients was only logical and fair."

I asked, "Had he already made the change before you saw him that day?"

"I wasn't sure. So far I haven't been contacted by the insurance company, so I assume that he made the change. Ask his wife."

"Don't worry, I will."

"Are we done?" he snapped.

"One last thing. At what time was your meeting with Dr. Unger on Saturday, April 14?"

"On weekends, I don't keep track of time," he said, and I felt myself dismissed.

People were in the process of setting up rows of folding chairs in the huge conference room and placing snacks and refreshments on a table to one side as I passed through, obviously getting ready for a gathering. As I was driving out of the Astute parking lot, a steady flow of cars made their way in.

For a second I worried that Dr. König might check me out on the internet and discover my true profession. Not a chance, I determined. The man was too busy and way too sure of himself to bother.

CHAPTER 21

I called Brenda on that same evening. When asked if she was the beneficiary of her husband's life insurance policy, she got irate and said, "Yes, and you've got a nerve to imply that I killed him for the insurance money."

"I'm not suggesting any such thing," I said, and related the conversation I'd had with Konrad König.

At the end of it she said, "I told Jake years ago to make the change and assumed that he did. How typical of him to forget about something important like that. All he ever had on his mind were his research projects." I could hear the resentment in her voice as she uttered that last sentence.

"Did you submit a claim?"

"It's kind of up in the air."

"Meaning?"

"I can't find the paperwork," she said. "Jake must have kept it in one of his file cabinets in the guesthouse, and it's gone to ashes. I called the insurance company the other day and asked how to proceed without having the policy on hand. I'm waiting for them to get back to me."

"What is the name of the insurance company," I asked.

She hesitated for a second before giving it to me, and I commented, "That's a reputable company. You'll hear from them soon."

"I hope so. I can use the money. Without Jake as provider, I'll have a heck of a time making ends meet on my salary alone."

"Surely your husband must have put away some savings."

"Wrong. Other than his SEP IRA, he tossed any extra cash into financing his pet projects," she said, again unable to keep the bitterness out of her voice.

I was about to end the call when she asked, "What did you think of the 'emperor'?"

"The what? Oh, I get it! In my mind, I call him 'the king'. To be honest, I wasn't as impressed as he would have liked me to be."

"He may have the IQ of a genius, but in my opinion, he's full of hot air," Brenda remarked.

We both burst out laughing.

CHAPTER 22

It so happened that I knew someone who was a life insurance agent with the company that Brenda had mentioned. He was an old family friend by the name of Max, and I called him at work the next morning.

"Nice to hear from you, Tara," he said. "Are your folks enjoying life up there at the tip of California? And do you still have that big black cat? He's such a character with his high jumps and extra loud purring."

I had forgotten how chatty Max was and replied, "We're all good, including Midnight." I was not about to let him know about Dad's crisis.

"What can I do for you, other than hooking you up with life insurance?" he joked.

"I need a big favor. Can you look up the beneficiary of Dr. Jake Unger's life insurance policy with your company?"

He whispered, "You're tackling insurance fraud in one of your articles?"

"Don't worry! This concerns a private matter and has nothing whatsoever to do with my job or my columns. And rest assured, insurance fraud is not the issue. I simply would like to know who the policy beneficiary is."

Again lowering his voice he said, "Policy content is confidential."

"I know, but the information is extremely important to me. I'd be eternally grateful if you could bend the rules a bit."

"You're making a highly unorthodox request, and looking into this could get me in deep trouble," he murmured.

"It's a matter of life and death!"

Not without humor he stated, "Life insurance always comes down to that."

"Please, Max!"

"I'll see what I can do. What's the name again?"

"Dr. Jake Unger. He passed away in April of this year. Thank you so much in advance, I owe you big time!"

"I haven't done anything yet, so don't get your hopes up too high. I'll get in touch with you if I find the information," he whispered, ending the call.

CHAPTER 23

On Saturday, June 23, I drove to the nursing home in Pasadena to see Oma. I tried to get there every couple of weeks but it had been almost a month already, so I was overdue. My German-born maternal grandmother was no longer herself these days, and I tended to be emotionally drained after each visit.

When my parents had moved to Northern California several years ago, they felt that it was best for Oma to stay in Pasadena, where she was happy in the retirement community of her choosing, rather than move her to new surroundings. She had made friends with other residents, and enjoyed some of the activities offered, like BINGO, nature walks, exercise classes, and movies. So she had lived a relatively active lifestyle, at least for a while.

When Oma had started showing signs of short-term memory loss, she was examined and diagnosed with early-stage Alzheimer's disease. At that time the disorder was mild, and she could stay in the independent part of the facility. In those days, she liked to reminisce about the past, and I enjoyed listening to her stories of when I was a little girl, and even farther back, when Mom was growing up. As her condition progressed, she moved to the assisted living wing of the retirement home.

I love Oma. As a child and teenager she had always been there for me. When Opa was alive, he and Oma took me on trips to their cabin in Big Bear Lake. Those were glorious days; boating in the summer and skiing in the winter. I owed a lot to her.

Like I mentioned, at first my visits were a pleasure for us both, but lately, my dropping by was sorrowful. It became hard for me to see my vibrant Oma having turned into a withdrawn old lady, who no longer seemed to know me. She had good days and bad days. On the good, she smiled and on the bad, she wept.

I signed in at the reception desk and was told to wait. Soon, Oma's caregiver appeared and said, "Hello, Ms Blunt! I've finished bathing your grandmother. You may see her now. She's in her room." And she added cheerfully, "She is having a good day today but isn't showing much of an appetite lately. We can hardly get her to eat."

Oma was sitting in a straight-back chair, looking out a window. She didn't turn around as I stepped into her room, seeming not to hear me.

I went over and touched her lightly on the arm, saying, "It's me, Tara."

She slowly turned her head, and I embraced her, not knowing if she recognized me or not.

I said, "Let's take a walk in the garden."

Without a word, she got up from the chair, we linked arms and then walked out her door, along the long corridor, and exited through a side entrance. Outside, on the fenced-in property, we went through the same routine we always did. We strolled along the path and stopped briefly at the hummingbird feeder hanging from a tree. If we were lucky, we'd see one of the birds hovering in mid-air, wings flapping like tiny propellers, with its long bill reaching into the feeder to extract nectar. On that particular day, though, no hummingbird flew by to get nourishment.

Next we came to another standstill by the small water fountain, then walked over to the flower garden, where Oma always reached up and touched one of the sunflowers, if in bloom. We eventually settled on what I presumed to be Oma's favorite bench in the shade of a Juniper tree.

There were a few residents walking about and enjoying the mild June weather, some in relatively good physical shape, and others on walkers or in wheelchairs. Some of these old folks acknowledged us with a greeting but most did not and seemed in a world of their own.

Although I didn't think that Oma recognized me as her grandchild, I came to the realization that she liked my company and enjoyed listening to me, even though I doubted that she understood much of what I said. She herself said little, and when she did talk, it didn't always make sense. My voice seemed to soothe her, so I had long made it a habit to chatter away about anything that came into my head while I was with her.

On that day I said, "You need to eat more."

"Eat," she repeated.

"You're getting way too skinny."

"Too skinny," she said.

Suddenly, Brenda's little Logan came to mind. He had also repeated words the way Oma did now. Was it possible that eventually, if we lived long enough, we would all be reverting to the toddler stage?

Then I went into a long spiel, which I'm sure she didn't comprehend, but there was a little smile on her lips as she listened. I started with, "I'm pretending to be a private investigator these days. Isn't that a hoot? A man got killed in an explosion and I don't think that it was by accident. I'm afraid that he was murdered."

I went into great detail about the Jake Unger tragedy and what I'd discovered so far, telling her that the whole thing was a big, complicated puzzle for me to solve.

After about twenty minutes of my detective tale, I switched over to something else and said, "Guess what? My dad, your son-in-law, bought a motorcycle and is riding around the country on it, as we speak."

"*Motorrad,*" she said.

"Yes," I exclaimed, "a motorcycle is a Motorrad in German. You *do* understand!" And I kissed her on both cheeks. She seemed taken aback for a second, then returned the sentiment and gave me a big hug of her own.

As she started to look weary, I realized that I must have tired her out. And when she got to her feet, I knew for sure that she wanted to go back inside.

On the drive back to Huntington Beach, I thought, the thing with the motorcycle was a surprise. Perhaps Oma understood more than I gave her credit for.

CHAPTER 24

On Sunday afternoon, I decided to stroll around the beautiful setting of Huntington Beach Central Park. It is located about a mile inland from the ocean on Goldenwest Street. The entire park is 350 acres large and has something to offer for everyone. There is a Senior Center and a Nature Center with native plants as well as oak and redwood trees attracting all kinds of birds. Picnic areas are set up along a natural lake, and weddings often take place in or around a gazebo.

Central Park also has a large Equestrian Center, but one of my favorite attractions is the Frisbee golf course, where I've spent many fun times playing with disc golf enthusiast friends.

On that particular Sunday, I strolled around the lake, watching ducks swimming and anglers trying to catch catfish. Although I enjoyed nature all around me, my thoughts were in detective mode. I mulled over what I had learned from talking to each person. Funny how nobody appeared to have paid attention to what time they had seen Jake on the day of the explosion. Brenda couldn't remember in what order her husband's visitors had shown up, and since the guys themselves did not know, or would not tell me, at what time they entered Jake's guesthouse, I was at a loss to figure out the sequence in which they came and went. Yet the order was extremely important. Except if the explosion was triggered by remote control, which was highly unlikely, the guilty person would have been the last visitor.

I knew that Julien had gone to see Jake in the morning and that all others - - Bryan Unger, Rob Cloud, and Konrad König - - had met him in the afternoon. In which order, though, I had no way of finding out, unless I stumbled on it by pure accident. I tried to recall what Brenda said when I talked to her on Sunday, the day after the tragedy. It was something like "People were coming and going. You'd think it was Grand Central Station." And then she made a remark about running errands, and that she had no idea who else had come by while she was gone, besides the people she had mentioned. What a weird comment! Did she suspect or know of anyone else having shown up that afternoon?

If so, it meant that the killer could be someone other than the individuals I had interviewed so far. Even if I asked Brenda to give me a list of all the people Jake had known - - an insane idea, to be sure - - it would be like searching for a needle in a haystack. And if she had someone in mind with that remark, I couldn't force her to reveal the person's name. It was possible that she had tried to protect that someone, but then why mention it at all?

This is not getting me any further with the investigation, I thought, and tried to put it out of my mind while concentrating on enjoying Central Park.

CHAPTER 25

Max called from his cellphone on Monday and said, "I'm on my lunch break. I didn't dare call you while at my desk."

I could hear traffic noise in the background and figured that our conversation would be confidential.

"Did you find the information on the policy in question?" I asked.

"Yes, and there seems to be a problem."

He hesitated and I sensed that he was reluctant to give me the information. I said, "Whatever you tell me will go no further."

He cleared his throat, then finally stated, "Dr. Jake Unger called our company Friday, April 13, asking to change the name from the current beneficiary, Konrad König, to his wife, Brenda Unger. One of our employees told him that we needed to have the request in writing in order to proceed, and Dr. Jake Unger said that he would send it to us per US mail right away. We never received it."

He continued, "At the beginning of this month, June 7 to be exact, Brenda Unger informed us that her husband had passed away and that she wanted to submit a claim but could not find the policy."

"Yes, I know that, Brenda said so herself," I commented, impatiently. "Now tell me who the legal beneficiary is."

"Since we never received anything in writing, Konrad König is the legitimate beneficiary as of today."

"But your company is holding off paying him?"

"You're quick, Tara! Yes, under the circumstances we're delaying the process. The letter may have gotten lost en route, for all we know, and may still show up. Also, we sense a lawsuit coming and have to be cautious."

Or the letter had been burned to ashes, I thought.

Aloud I said, "Thank you so much! I owe you big time."

Max reminded, "You said this was a private matter, and it's best if I don't know the reason for your request. But do I have your word that you'll keep it to yourself and out of your columns now and forever?"

"Absolutely!"

"I could get fired over this, you know."

"I can well imagine. You have my word, Max."

CHAPTER 26

Wondering about that unknown person who might have been seeking out Jake on his fateful day did not leave me any peace. Maybe there existed a nosy neighbor who had paid attention. It was worth a try.

I found myself on the late Jake Unger's street once again in the early evening before dusk. A next-door neighbor was getting home from work, and I caught her checking her mailbox. When asked if she had noticed people coming to or leaving the Ungers' residence prior to the explosion on April 14, the woman told me that she and her family had been out of town on that weekend. She had heard about the tragic event after the fact and was sorry for not being able to help me. To my question of how well she knew her neighbors, she replied, "Not well at all. We only moved here last November."

The neighbor on the other side of the Unger bungalow proved to be more productive. I rang the doorbell to the three-story house and waited for what seemed a long time. Either there was no one home or else they chose not to answer, I thought. About to ring the bell again, I withdrew my finger in mid-air as the door was flung open by a man. I recognized him as the onlooker I had talked to when I'd arrived to get a peek at Jake's lab, only to find the place ablaze. I hoped that the man would not recognize me. Distinct piano playing sounded out of a room on the first floor. If I was not mistaken, the piece was by Grieg.

I started my pitch about investigating the incident of the explosion, and he said, "So you're a private eye! When I saw you that day I figured you might be a reporter who got tipped off about the fire. Come on in, then." So much for not having been recognized, I thought.

I followed him into the foyer where he looked at me with inquisitive eyes and remarked, "Come to think of it, you must have already been investigating the case even then. That would have explained your arrival at the scene."

I let him believe that and said, "So you remember the day of the explosion well?"

"I'll never forget it," he assured me.

His answer gave me a perfect opening to inquire about people he might have noticed visiting his neighbor on that day prior to the fire.

He stated, "I'm a freelance graphic design artist. Like most other days, I spent that Saturday up on the third floor in my studio and didn't pay much attention to anything but my work."

"Is there anyone else in your household who might have noticed people dropping in on Dr. Unger at his lab?"

"My wife was not home that afternoon, so she couldn't help you either."

I was trying to come up with another question when he declared, "Oh, I just remembered something. I don't have a view from my studio to the front of the Ungers' house, nor did I have one to the entrance of their detached guesthouse on the day in question. At the time, I could only see down to their garage and the side of the little structure from my window. When I looked down, I observed a person standing between the garage and the guesthouse, peeking in through a side window."

"Did you think that was odd?"

"Not at the time. I figured that there was nobody home in the bungalow and the person checked if someone was in the guesthouse, and if yes, I assumed he would go around to its front door."

"But you thought it weird later?" I inquired.

"Yes, since afterward the Unger woman and her little boy went to the garage, and I saw her drive away. So she'd obviously been home when the person looked into the guesthouse."

"It was a man?"

"He was wearing a baseball cap, so I assumed it was a man but it could've been a woman."

I asked, "Did you see the person getting admitted to the guesthouse?"

"No, I didn't have a view to the front of it from my window. Come, let me show you," he said, and I followed him up two flights of stairs.

The sound of piano playing was barely audible as we entered the studio on the third floor. A huge monitor flanked by a smaller one on each side hovered over a large desk. I noticed a Wacom tablet alongside the keyboard. A good-size drawing board stood next to the desk, and a collection of print finishes and high-end design collateral were propped up against one wall. There was a library of design volumes, among them a Pantone color reference book. The window stretched along the entire length of the room, providing the place with strong natural lighting.

I said, "Your studio is impressive."

"It serves me well. I do both printed and digital designs."

Going over to the window, I looked down onto the backyard and garage next door and said, "You don't have a view down to the neighbors while sitting at your desk."

"Correct. On that day in April, I took a break and stretched by the window, something I do periodically to get a bit of exercise." And he pointed to the space next to the Ungers' garage and said, "That used to be the guesthouse, but as you can see, only the foundation remains."

I inquired, "Can you describe the person you saw looking into your neighbors' guesthouse other than that he or she wore a baseball cap?"

"Sorry. Looking down from this height I couldn't make out the person clearly. I can't even tell you whether the individual was tall, short, thin, or fat."

"I know this is hard to recall over two months later, but can you give me an idea of what time it was?"

He stated, "I can tell you exactly. I was checking the time often since I had a skype session scheduled for later that day. When I got up from my desk to stretch, it was 3:30. The person in question showed up a minute or two later."

"And at what time did you see Brenda Unger drive away?"

"Approximately fifteen minutes afterward. I was about ready to go to my desk and back to work."

I said, "I take it that you heard the explosion?"

"Did I ever! The noise was ear-piercing and the blast made my own house shake. At first, I couldn't tell from what direction the bang came from, and after smelling smoke, I looked out the window and saw the neighbors' guesthouse in flames. I called 911 and hoped to God that Dr. Unger was not in his laboratory."

"So you were the neighbor who called the authorities. At what time was the explosion, by the way?"

"About five past four or so. Don't you have that documented?"

"Sure," I said, "just wanted to compare notes. By the way, did you inform the authorities of the person you spotted by the guesthouse?"

"Nobody asked me. Besides, until now when you came along, I assumed the explosion was accidental."

We went back down the stairs and heard the same piece of music being played. Whoever was practicing on the piano got stuck on one particular passage, going over it again and again. My escort seemed to guess what I was thinking and said, "My wife is a pianist and occasionally gives lessons to protégées."

I nodded in acknowledgment. At the bottom of the stairs I said, "One more thing. How well did you know Jake Unger?"

He replied, "During the three years since we've lived here, I didn't get to know him. In fact, I hardly ever saw him. He was a man who kept to himself. Brenda was more talkative. When we moved in, she introduced herself and explained that her husband was a physicist and kept a lab in the guesthouse, and that she was studying to become a dental hygienist. She was highly pregnant at the time and gave birth to her baby a couple of weeks later. I might add that the little boy is extremely quiet; we never hear him cry."

And with finality he stated, "That's about all my wife and I learned about our neighbors in the bungalow next door."

He walked me back to the front door, where I said, "You helped a lot. Thank you so much for your time," and left.

While walking to where I had parked my Honda it occurred to me that we had not exchanged names. I had not been interested in learning his, and I was glad that he did not ask for mine, or he could have googled me and found out who I really was.

CHAPTER 27

Following my workout at the gym early Tuesday morning, June 26, I got a glimpse of the trainer I had spotted in a tête-à-tête with Brenda two weeks earlier. He was teaching a body pump class. On my way out, I stopped at the front desk and asked, "What's the name of the instructor of your body pump workout?"

"That would be Jeff Moody," the receptionist replied.

"I understand that he's also a personal trainer. I'm thinking of hiring him. May I have his number?"

"No problem," she said, and handed it to me. I called later from home and made an appointment to see him. He fitted me in between clients in the afternoon of the next day.

The rest of that Tuesday I had designated to getting some work done. While doing research for an article I was writing on bird migration, I was interrupted twice by phone calls. Although I hated the intrusions while concentrating on my subject matter, I answered them.

The first was from Mom. She said, "Your dad sent me a postcard from El Paso. Can you believe it, a postcard?"

"He's making good time and seems to keep to his road plan on Interstate 10. And now you know that he got to El Paso all in one piece." I replied.

"That's not funny, Tara!"

"Sorry, Mom, I'm just trying to cheer you up." I did get a snicker out of her when I asked, "How's your love life, by the way?"

"I'm undecided between choosing the nice young man in charge of the produce department at the local grocery store or the guy that walks his dog past our house every day."

Then she got serious and asked, "Have you been to Pasadena lately?"

"I went for a visit last Saturday."

"How is she?"

"The same," I replied.

Mom sighed and said, "I should make an effort and get down to see her more often."

"Yes, you should!"

On that note we ended the call.

The trouble with Mom was that she had a tendency to burst into tears during her visits. Oma may not have been aware of their mother/daughter relationship, but she was susceptible to vibes. Outbursts of any kind - - sadness, anger, or even loud laughter - - made her feel agitated. Mom knew this but was unable to control her emotions.

Julien phoned next and inquired, "How's the sleuthing coming along?"

I said, "I've interviewed numerous people and determined that every single suspect has a motive, but I can't single anyone out as yet." And I went down the list, naming everyone I had talked with.

"Did they all accept you as being a PI and cooperate?" Julien wanted to know.

"Mostly. I have my doubts about Konrad König, who appeared suspicious. Still, I was able to drag the information I wanted out of him."

"Good for you."

I remarked, "I found Rob Cloud a bit odd."

"He's a strange recluse all right, full of weird habits and quirks. But I got used to him when rooming together."

"The man seemed to have an aversion to shaking my hand."

"Oh that! Rob is also a germ freak and doesn't like to touch people."

"That explains it."

Julien asked, "So what's next on your detective agenda?"

"Tomorrow I'm scheduled to talk with Brenda's boyfriend, Jeff Moody, and then I'll do some major reasoning and deliberating."

"How did you figure out her lover's name?"

"I have my ways," I said.

I heard his slight chuckle. Then he inquired, "Have you given the Paris vacation some more thought?"

"Sorry, it hasn't entered my mind lately."

"We could ask for separate rooms, if you wish."

"I'll think about it after the Jake Unger business is settled. At the moment, I can't concentrate on anything else."

"Fair enough. There is no time limit on the trip I won."

"What have *you* been up to?" I asked.

"Mainly, I'm preoccupied with searching for the perfect rental space for my new lab. I've looked at many places in the Long Beach area but haven't found the ideal one yet. They're either too small or else not suitable for laboratory use."

"Keep at it; you'll find the perfect spot, I'm sure."

I was ready to end the call when he said, "About that reasoning and deliberating you mentioned. Two heads are better than one."

"What are you suggesting?"

"We could plan an outing and logically discuss your investigation. Who knows, we may come up with results."

"I'll think about that too," I said.

CHAPTER 28

On Wednesday afternoon, June 27, I turned up at the gym at the appointed time, wearing what I had long labeled my detective outfit: a gray tailored suit with the skirt reaching just above the knee and red heels to add some color.

I was told to wait in Jeff Moody's office and that he would be with me shortly. Calling the cubbyhole I sat in an "office," was a stretch. The nook was about 6 foot square, barely large enough to accommodate the small desk and two chairs it housed. There was no window. On the wall behind the desk hung a framed photograph showing an athlete crossing the finish line at a triathlon. On close examination, I recognized the runner as the trainer I was waiting for.

I started to get claustrophobic when the man arrived in the flesh. After introductions, he looked at my outfit and said, "I was going to walk you through some basic routines, but you obviously didn't come prepared to work out. So today we can discuss what your goals are and then start getting to work on the day of your first session. I can explain the different programs we offer, or let me know if you have a specific training in mind." He looked at me expectantly as his speech came to a halt.

I said, "You've got it all wrong. I'm here to interview *you*."

He gave me a blank stare.

"I'm investigating the explosion and death of Dr. Unger."

He burst out, "You are a conniving piece of work! They specifically told me at the front desk that you want to hire me as your trainer."

"Would you have agreed to talk with me had I stated my business?"

"Probably not," he said. And he suddenly smiled, evidently seeing the humor in it. The turnaround didn't last, however, and he stated, "I don't know anything about any explosion or someone's death."

"You do know Brenda Unger, the victim's widow, rather well."

"Brenda is in a couple of classes I teach. So yes, I know her. But not 'rather well' like you said."

"Don't play games, Mr. Moody. I have it from two separate sources that Brenda Unger and you are romantically involved."

He realized that there was no point in denying it and immediately went into attack mode, saying, "You must be the reporter woman Brenda told me about who's snooping around. You're ..."

"Columnist, not reporter," I interjected.

"Whatever! You're wasting everyone's time, including your own. Brenda's husband messed around with hazardous material once too often and blew his lab and himself up. That's what happened, period. Trying to make a murder investigation out of it is absurd."

"So you've met Jake Unger?" I asked.

"No, but Brenda told me that he was always working on some project or other, using toxic chemicals."

"How long have you been carrying on the affair?"

"That's none of your business, and I don't see what it has to do with your so-called investigation."

He reconsidered and said. "But I'm a good sport. I've dated Brenda for a little over a year now." And he added, "If her husband hadn't spent day and night in his precious lab and paid more attention to her, it would've never come to it in the first place."

I said, "Where were you on Saturday around 3:30 p.m., April 14, the day of the explosion?"

"You want my alibi? That's ridiculous."

"Possibly, but I'd still like to know."

He stated, "I work here at the gym every other Saturday. I don't remember the April schedule and would need to look it up."

"Please do."

He rolled his eyes and then checked the data on his laptop. After retrieving the information with a few clicks, he said, "I was off on April 14."

"So my question stands, where were you around 3:30 in the afternoon on that Saturday?"

"I don't remember."

I said, "What if I told you that someone saw you standing by the Ungers' guesthouse, peeking in through a window?"

"I'd say that person is a liar," he replied, slamming his fist down onto the desk.

"In that case, you have nothing to worry about."

He stared me down, then checked his watch and got up, stating, "I'm scheduled to see an *actual* client. Is that all?"

I got to my feet also, glad to leave the suffocating pigeonhole, and thanked him for his time and cooperation. We were both getting out the door when I reached into my purse for a business card and, handing it to him, said, "Give me a call if you remember your whereabouts of April 14 at 3:30 p.m."

CHAPTER 29

That evening, as Midnight and I were getting comfortable on my couch, and I was looking forward to watching a movie I had purchased ages ago, the phone rang. I let the answering machine pick up.

I heard Brenda's angry voice shout, "Get to the phone if you're home!"

For a brief moment I was considering ignoring her command but changed my mind and answered.

"I'm here," I said. "What's up?"

"You know damn well what's up! How dare you interrogate Jeff and accuse him of causing the explosion. He had nothing to do with it. Anyone who claims he was at the guesthouse is lying. Just because he can't remember what he did that day doesn't make him the guilty person."

In the same breath she continued, "How did you even know about us? I'm 100 percent sure that I never mentioned Jeff during our talks. I'm really pissed and wished I had never laid eyes on you, let alone agreed for you to play the detective. I could kick myself for having invited you into my house on that miserable day you showed up out of the blue. At first, you came across as this caring, wanting to set things right person, and now I realize that you're not as harmless as you pretend. I thought that if Jake was murdered like you made me believe, I owed it to him to get justice. He was good to me - - at least in the beginning. Now that you're attacking Jeff, I'm no longer buying your crap."

She finally inhaled, and I said, "I didn't accuse your boyfriend of any crime. If he was under that impression, tell him that he's mistaken. In order to conduct the investigation properly, I have to look at all possibilities. As far as knowing about your relationship with Jeff Moody, I first learned it from a reliable source, which I'm not at liberty to reveal. And then I saw you two together in the hallway of the gym one day after I'd finished my workout. You both were too preoccupied with your own issues to pay any attention to me."

"So you've been spying on us and listening to our conversation?"

"From your point of view that's what it amounts to," I admitted.

"Well, you've got some nerve! You must have suspected me as the bad guy all along, and now you're dragging Jeff into the picture as my accomplice. Let me tell you, there is such a thing as slander, and I may go ahead and hire a lawyer to sue you for it."

Her threat was silly and evoked a sudden urge to laugh in me, but I suppressed it. No sense in making her even angrier.

I said, "I'm far from accusing you or anyone else of being responsible for the explosion. I do need to treat all persons concerned as suspects. I haven't singled you out in any way, so your rage is unjustified."

She seemed to calm down and said, "So leave Jeff out of it. He's not one of your 'persons concerned'." And without much ceremony, she cut the line.

On the heels of her ranting, I had lost all desire to watch the movie and instead concentrated on the real life drama I had involved myself in. Brenda was obviously upset that I knew about her affair but that wasn't all. Her anger had gone deeper. I was certain of that.

Perhaps I had misinterpreted the remark she had made during our initial chat that "God only knew who else had shown up to talk to her husband that day." At the time I thought she either knew of someone other than the people she had already mentioned - - maybe a stranger to her - - who had paid him a visit, or that she made that mystery person up in order to take the limelight away from herself. Later, I had speculated that the un-named individual could have been her boyfriend, whom she wished to protect.

Now it occurred to me that none of the above may have been true. It was possible that Brenda had made the remark simply as a matter of speech, meaning, "Who knew? More people could have come to see him that afternoon." On the other hand, it was a fact that her graphic design artist neighbor had seen a person sneak a look through the guesthouse window around 3:30 that Saturday afternoon. That could have been the mystery person, or it may have been one of the individuals that Brenda had originally named. If the latter, it all boiled down again to the order in which these people had come to see Jake Unger.

One thing was clear, Brenda's heated outburst directed at me came out of her attempt to shield and protect Jeff Moody. Why did she think he needed protecting? I wondered. Trying to put myself into her shoes, I thought, would I have reacted in the same way? Not a chance. Most likely, I would not have made that phone call and instead let things run their course. Guilty or not, drawing attention to myself and my boyfriend would be the last thing I'd have wished to do. Temperamental Brenda hadn't thought things through when she made that call to me.

Not for the first time I mulled over the interviews I'd had with each suspect to no avail. All had plausible motives for wanting Jake Unger out of the way, and as far as I could tell, each had the opportunity to set the explosion in motion. But for the life of me, I could not narrow it down to one person. I should have been able to get an idea by now but seemed no closer to solving the murder, if indeed it was murder, than when I'd started the investigation.

Midnight must have sensed my frustration and jumped off my lap in search of a more pleasant spot. As the evening progressed and I got more irritated by the minute, I decided to take Julien up on his offer to help. Like he'd said, two heads were better than one.

CHAPTER 30

We picked Friday, June 29, for our collaboration meeting, and since Julien had never been there, we settled on a walk around Balboa Island. I made it clear to him that this wasn't a date. I simply needed his input concerning my Jake Unger investigation.

We drove to the Balboa Peninsula in separate cars. The weather was perfect: upper seventies and sunny. I had debated whether to wear jeans or shorts, but shorts won. When we met at the Balboa Pier parking lot at 10:30 a.m., I noticed that Julien had made the same wardrobe choice. We walked the short stretch along Main Street that led to the fun zone, where we passed arcades, beach boutiques, eateries, and boat rentals.

As we came by the Ferris wheel, I said, "I can't believe you've never been here. I assumed that everyone living in Southern California has been to Balboa."

"Oh, I've been to Newport and Balboa a few times but never made it to the island."

"Well, it's charming. You'll see."

We went on board the ferryboat that accommodated three cars, a few bicycles, and about a dozen passengers on foot. During the crossing, which took but a few minutes, I became a tour guide.

I said, "Besides the ferry, the island is also accessible via a northeast bridge and several public docks. There are approximately 3000 residents living on 0.2 square miles, giving the place a high population density. Although extremely expensive, the houses stand on small lots of 30 x 85 feet. Marine Avenue, the main drag, consists of small businesses, like restaurants, bakeries, and boutiques. The island has its own post office and fire station."

Julien appeared amused and asked, "Did you google these facts to impress me, or are you in the market to purchase property on the island?"

"Touché! For your information, I researched Balboa Island a while back for one of my environmental articles."

Once we arrived at our destination, we started off on the paved pedestrian boardwalk, with delightful small homes to our left and the waterfront to the right. Anchored small boats swayed gently in the breeze. I suggested walking the perimeter of the isle along the path, which gave us plenty of privacy to hold our discussion. There were people ahead and behind us strolling along, and some coming from the opposite direction. A few paces in front of us, an adorable Chihuahua peeked out of a young man's backpack, causing folks to make enthusiastic comments on passing, but nobody paid any attention to us. Time to get down to the purpose of our outing, I determined.

CHAPTER 31

I gave Julien a brief summary of the interviews I'd had with each suspect and what I'd learned from the Ungers' neighbor, and also the info I had received from Max, my insurance agent friend. Brenda's outburst over the phone I kept to myself. No need to expose her ranting, I decided.

He listened carefully and then suggested, "Let's take each person into consideration, one by one."

And so we did, starting with Brenda Unger.

I said, "One thing is clear. She was unhappy in the marriage."

"Surely that was no reason to kill her husband. Much easier to just divorce him," Julien pointed out.

"You're forgetting about the life insurance policy."

"Didn't you say that König was the beneficiary?"

"True, but Brenda didn't know that at the time and was under the impression that Jake had changed it to benefit her."

"Okay," he said, "she had a motive. What about opportunity?"

"There's a slight chance that she was that mystery person the neighbor observed peeping into the guesthouse. According to him that was at 3:30, and at roughly 3:45, he noticed her driving away. So if she is our culprit, that would've given her approximately fifteen minutes to knock Jake unconscious and set things in motion for the explosion. The neighbor said that the time of the big bang was around 4:05, which is about right, since I came upon the scene a little less than half an hour later.

"By the way, the firefighters must have arrived in record time and done a tremendous job of putting out the fire. When I got there, they had the flames contained before giving them a chance to spread to the main house."

Julien said, "Timewise it would fit, but there's a flaw in your reasoning. Why would Brenda peek through the window? She must have already known that Jake was there, and even if she didn't, the natural thing would be to go straight to the front door of the guesthouse."

I took a moment to think and then said, "What if she wanted to check what he was doing? My guess is that only a surprise attack would work in her case. So she may have wanted to make sure he was concentrating on his work with his back to the door before she entered."

"That scenario is plausible," he agreed. "In that case Brenda had motive as well as opportunity."

We had arrived at Marine Avenue and I inquired, "Do you want to stroll down the main drag and look at shops or stay on the boardwalk and go around the outside of the island?"

Julien looked in both directions and replied, "I'd like to keep going on the path where there are less people and distractions." And he asked, "Who's next?"

I said, "Let's stay with the family and tackle Bryan Unger. There was not much love between the siblings, and I gathered that Bryan was jealous of his highly intelligent older brother. Bryan and Brenda don't get along either, but that's beside the point. The motive, in my opinion, is simple greed, however. In order to get rich, Bryan needed the sale of his parents' house to become a reality. He knew that it would never happen while his brother was alive. He thinks that he has a right to force Brenda to sell it now. What the actual legalities are does not concern us. The important thing is that Bryan thought so, and therefore we have the motive."

Julien took over and said, "And now to opportunity. Since we don't know in what order people showed up, any one of your suspects could be the mystery guest. Let's call him or her 'X'. We established that X was the last person to see Jake before the explosion and logically must be the killer. So Bryan Unger may well have been X."

Rob Cloud was next on our agenda to be scrutinized. I said, "Like I've already told you before, I found the man a bit odd. Did you know that he was seeing a psychiatrist?"

"No, but I'm not surprised."

"Are you suggesting that he is mentally unstable?"

"It's a possibility."

"Anyhow," I continued, "the psychiatrist told him to socialize more, which he obviously took to heart. He claimed to have made peace with Jake Unger and that they'd parted as friends, but I'm not positive he told the truth. According to him, his former roommate had been a brilliant physicist but was stubborn as a mule."

Julien chuckled and remarked, "Rob got that one right!"

"To the question of motive: Even if unbalanced, he still needed to have a reason to kill. A couple things come to mind. The two might have had another of their heated theory fights, and Rob lost his head. Or, more likely, Jake refused to put in a good word for him with Konrad König, so that his chances of becoming a member of Astute were slim."

Julien said, "That's plausible. Rob always had a fixed mind about things, and if the shrink told him to go out and mingle, he may have become obsessed with the idea."

I suddenly remembered something and said, "In the course of our interview, Rob mentioned being under the impression that Jake seemed to want to rush him out of the guesthouse by frequently checking his watch. Konrad König informed me that Jake specifically asked him to come by, which makes me think that Rob was there before König."

"Are you telling me that we can eliminate Rob as the villain since, in that case, he couldn't be the X person?"

"No, we can't. Konrad König may have been lying or there may have been another reason Jake wanted Rob to leave."

Julien suggested, "A good reason could've been that Jake was in the middle of something when Rob turned up and in a hurry to get back to his lab and continue with his project. Knowing Jake, I can picture that scenario."

He stated, "So we can add Rob Cloud to the list of people who had motive and opportunity."

At that point we were more or less at the halfway mark of our stroll around the island. We stood still to admire a life-size bronze mermaid statue in someone's front yard.

Julien remarked, "These homes are by no means large, but they're extremely interesting."

"Bigger isn't always better," I agreed.

Then we reverted to the subject at hand and took Konrad König into consideration.

I said, "I understand that Jake admired California's top man of Astute. During my interview with the commander in charge, I formed my own opinion, but I'd like to know what you thought of him."

Without any qualms he replied, "It's a well-known fact that Konrad König is a genius, but personally, I think he's full of himself."

"Good," I said, "we're on the same page then. Now let's talk motive. König was the beneficiary of Jake's life insurance policy. During our talk, he said he didn't know whether Jake had already made the change to benefit Brenda. This is speculation, but what if Jake told him that the written request was ready to be mailed to the insurance company? König may have even seen the envelope. So he quickly formed his devilish plan to murder Jake and at the same time blow up the letter that would change the beneficiary."

Julien put in, "And if Jake wanted to talk to him first before making the change, the result would be the same. He'd have to silence him."

"One thing, though, speaks for his innocence: He brought up the subject of the life insurance himself."

"He knew that would become public sooner or later. Admitting that the insurance policy was the purpose of his visit to Jake on the day of the explosion was a smart move on his part."

"He's a genius, after all!" I said. "And as far as opportunity, he could very well be X."

That left Jeff Moody as our last suspect.

Julien suggested, "Where lover boy is concerned, he may have been in cahoots with Brenda and followed her orders or else acted on his own, with her having no idea what he was up to. Either way, his motive would be to get rid of his rival and at the same time help Brenda collect the life insurance money he thought was due her."

I chimed in, "As to opportunity, he didn't work at the gym that day and couldn't tell me where he was at 3:30 in the afternoon. If he is X and Brenda's accomplice, she may have told him to time the explosion to when she was running her errands, creating an alibi for herself."

"Yes, that makes sense."

My list of suspects to consider and deliberate on was thus exhausted. At about the same time we had come full circle of the island. I tried hard not to show my disappointment. Going over the facts with Julien had been stimulating and thought provoking but had left me no closer to solving the mystery.

On the ferryboat taking us back to the peninsula Julien remarked, "You're awfully quiet. You must have expected better results from our teamwork."

"You said it! I'm back to square one," I admitted.

CHAPTER 32

By the time we walked toward the ocean on Main Street, we were starved, so we stopped at a Mexican restaurant for lunch, located at the very end of the road, right off the beach.

We obtained a table by the window with an ocean view. While sipping Margaritas and waiting for our orders of nachos to arrive, Julien touched my hand lightly and said, "Don't worry. You'll figure it out in the end."

Disgusted with myself, I said, "I should have left it alone. The whole thing is none of my business. Besides, I'm starting to think that I'm wrong. The explosion may have been nothing but an unfortunate accident."

Julien said, "That's possible, of course. Remember when you first told me that you suspected foul play, I mentioned that Jake may have been absent-minded and placed the ammonium nitrate too close to the heat lamp."

"Yea, I remember. And if that's the case, I've wasted everyone's time and got people upset for no good reason."

At that moment the waitress sat two plates with mountains of nachos, topped with hot sauce in front of us. She also provided extra paper napkins as a precaution for the messy finger food.

Julien said, "Let's not talk about it any longer and enjoy our meal."

The tasty food and margarita did the job. Soon, I was able to get Jake Unger out of my mind and concentrate on my appetite.

Between bites Julien asked, "So what are you up to when not working or sleuthing?"

"Nothing much. I work out at the gym Tuesdays and Thursdays and go for early morning walks all other days."

"No wonder you keep in such good shape."

I looked out the window and noticed a wedding party posing for pictures on the beach. The bride and bridesmaids had taken their shoes off and waded through the sand, holding their pumps in one hand and pulling up their gowns with the other.

Turning back to Julien I asked, "Have you ever been married?"

He shook his head and said, "I was engaged once, but she got cold feet and dumped me."

"Sorry."

"Nothing to be sorry about. I came to realize later that it wouldn't have worked anyhow. She was a high maintenance sort of woman."

The bride and groom posed for one last solo picture, and then the entire party walked away from the ocean toward our restaurant. As they got closer, I saw that they were all very young, in their teens, I guessed. With a gesture in their direction, I said, "I hope it works out for them."

"What about you?" Julien asked, "Did you ever tie the knot?"

"Not a chance, but I've had way too many bad relationships."

"I figured as much." And after a pause he asked, "And now you're gun-shy?"

"You've got that right. My grandmother, who used to be full of wisdom, would say, *"Gebrannte Kinder fürchten das Feuer."*

"Translation, please. I don't speak German."

"It means, burnt children fear the fire."

He asked, "Did your grandmother pass away?"

"No, but she's no longer herself," I replied.

He must have sensed my sadness and stayed silent, touching my hand again ever so gently.

The moment passed quickly and then he said, "So you speak fluent German?"

"I speak some but wouldn't call it fluent."

He remarked, "How about brushing up on your French? I understand Paris is delightful in the summer."

I gave him an angry glare and exclaimed, "Don't pressure me, dammit."

"Sorry," he said, "That was uncalled for. I won't bring it up anymore. You tell me when you're ready to discuss the trip."

If ever, I thought. Aloud I said, "It's a deal."

We were both a bit tongue-tied after that altercation, had finished the meal, and were ready to call it quits for the day.

As we walked over to the pier parking lot, Julien said, "Thanks for introducing me to Balboa Island. I enjoyed your company. Too bad that we didn't make much progress in your investigation, but I do think that we make a good team."

I said, "Thanks for coming. We haven't solved the crime, but at least you helped sort things out. The rest is up to me to mull over."

When we got to my Honda, he gave me a thumbs-up, bent down to kiss my forehead, and then hurriedly walked to where his own car was parked.

CHAPTER 33

Coming back from my brisk walk around the neighborhood early Saturday morning, I almost made it past Mr. A's door undetected when he flung it open and beamed, "A good morning to you, Tara! Where have you been hiding? Remember, we still need to do that interview before you can work on the write-up about my shop."

"I didn't forget, but I'm extremely busy these days," I said, while passing him and heading up the flight of stairs.

"Just checking. Have a nice weekend!" he called after me, but by that time I was already at my own door.

I decided to treat myself to a bubble bath. While soaking in the tub minutes later, I thought, go ahead and get it over with. So what if antiques are not something I'd normally concern myself with? A bit of time spent in Mr. A's shop and listening to what he has to say about his treasures won't kill me. Writing the actual column will be a cinch, since there's hardly any research involved. And I know just the magazine I could pitch the piece to.

Before long, I rang the man's doorbell, and when he answered it, I announced, "I've checked my calendar. I'm free to interview you next Tuesday, July 3. Are you going to be in your shop around two o'clock in the afternoon?"

He was overjoyed and said, "That's the day before Independence Day. I'll make sure to be there."

On that same morning, I got a text from my friend Crystal, who wanted to know what I was planning to wear that night. Oh no! We had tickets to see a musical which had totally slipped my mind.

As a result, I stood in front of my wardrobe closet checking the inventory. My mind made up, I texted her back with the following message, "Semi-formal, black and white. Dinner first, the usual. Pick you up at 5:30."

I was looking forward to the show with great eagerness and promised myself, *forget about Jake Unger for the entire weekend.*

My landline rang before I had barely finished that thought. Making an identity check, I saw the word "Astute." So much for giving the investigation a rest, I murmured to myself and took the call.

He didn't bother with any greeting and yelled, "You ought to be ashamed of yourself! Landing an interview with me under false pretenses. Don't you have any ethics?"

"Hello, Professor König! So you found me out."

"Precisely! I got behind with my reading, so it wasn't until today that I picked up the Science Kicks Magazine and stumbled upon your article on Dr. Julien Floyd and his invention of fully biodegradable packaging."

"Did you like the column?" I inquired.

"That's not the point. I'm calling to give you a piece of my mind."

He continued, "When I saw your name in print I knew right away that you're nothing but a shameless con artist. I mean, how many Tara Blunts could there be? When you came to Astute to talk with me, I had a vague idea that I'd seen you before. Now I remember exactly where and when. I saw you in line to chat with Dr. Floyd at the banquet held in his honor."

"All true," I stated, "but the interview request was not made under false pretenses. I *am* investigating the explosion at the Unger residence."

"On what authority, I'd like to know," he raged on. "I'm unfamiliar with what the legal consequences are for impersonating a private investigator. What I do know is that you shouldn't get away unpunished."

"Pardon me, sir, but I didn't impersonate anyone, nor did I claim to be a private eye. Don't accuse me of breaking any laws. I approached you stating my own name."

"Correct. But you tricked me into giving out information. That's deception in my book."

He was right in that last instance, no arguing there. Still, I wasn't about to take it lying down and said, "So I'm not a professional detective, but I do want to find the truth about what happened to Dr. Unger. Don't you feel the need for justice regarding your friend and fellow scientist?"

König replied, "As I told you when you extorted that interview from me and I'm telling you now, the idea that someone murdered Jake Unger is absurd. The explosion was a tragic accident, nothing more."

"I hope you're right."

"I *am* right, so stop this ridiculous investigation."

Having gotten all that out of his system, he ended the call. Again, the man did not bother with a polite formality of "goodbye."

I wondered, what did Konrad König intend to accomplish with this phone call other than ranting and raving? Telling me that he knows who I really am? I was unimportant to him and he wouldn't waste his time. Letting me know that he was aware of my deception? Again, not at all likely. The man was too busy teaching physics at a university and being the leader of the California Astute chapter to bother with taking the time to set me straight. No, the sole purpose of the call was an attempt at getting me to stop the investigation. Interesting! And did he succeed? Just the opposite, I answered my own question.

CHAPTER 34

A door chime announced me as I entered Mr. A's antique shop on Tuesday afternoon the next week. The man himself was busy helping a customer and in the process of unlocking a display cabinet.

After spotting me he hollered, "Be right with you, Tara!" which gave me a chance to browse through the place on my own.

On first glance, it appeared in total chaos. Unlike a contemporary department store where items were arranged by categories, here all goods were displayed in a jumble. Bronze sculptures, clocks, and glassware were heaped together with old toys, and there were boxes haphazardly placed throughout the shop. A large Tiffany lamp shade was surrounded by silver flatware and bowls. But that was by no means all the silver available. In a different section of the vast room, I noticed a set of sterling silver spoons, forks, and knives, and in yet another, a silver teapot stood proudly among a trio of ceramic vases.

Speaking of ceramics, on a table against the outer wall, I saw Doulton and Goldscheider figurines and, in another partition, I found Oriental ceramics. A brass desk lamp mounted on a snow marble base was placed amid old maps and old-fashioned black-and-white photos. There was a corner with vintage clothing and old books. On the walls hung paintings, mirrors, and posters, and from the ceiling dangled several chandeliers.

I was gazing into a glass display case with real and classic custom jewelry, when Mr. A tapped me on the shoulder and said, "Sorry about the delay. I'm all yours now."

"No problem. Business comes first," I said with a grin.

He guided me to the back of the store which was separated from the front by an arch. We passed his small open-door office, located between the two sections, and entered the rear.

I took one look and exclaimed, "There is law and order after all!"

"What do you mean?"

"You have nothing but furniture in this part of your store."

"Right," he said. "As you can see, I don't have too much room for furniture, so I'm selective in what I acquire and only choose the very best."

He proudly pointed out a George III mahogany and strung cylinder bureau and then walked me over to an early 19th Century provincial sideboard with a beech top and two cupboard doors.

"And now to my pride and joy," he announced, steering me to a remote corner of the room. Pointing to a small piece of furniture, he stated, "This is an 18th Century Italian Rococo walnut and gilt-metal mounted commode. Isn't it a beauty?"

The piece was nice, I thought, but since I had no understanding of nor interest in antique furniture, I could not appreciate its significance. I acknowledged his enthusiasm with a brief smile and nod.

Then I said, "Why hide this special piece in this far-off spot? Don't you want to sell it?"

He chuckled and admitted, "You see right through me! No doubt, I need to sell it eventually, but for now, I'd like to admire it a while longer." And he said, "Come, let's go into my office and do the interview."

After I had settled in a chair and faced him across an antique desk, I pulled a notebook from my bag, and our talk began. I first had him go into his background, which revealed some interesting new facts about my neighbor. Born of middle-aged parents and raised in Patras, Western Greece, Mr. A had originally been a pilot, flying commercial aircrafts. Even at that time, he had been interested in collecting antiques and had amassed a sizable personal collection. He had chosen the United States as his permanent residence and immigrated to New York City. Although he found Manhattan fascinating, he hated the cold winters of the East Coast and ended up settling in Southern California.

Then the airline company he worked for went out of business, and he was laid off. At that point in his life, he decided to turn his hobby into a profession, and with the inheritance money of his parents was able to set himself up in the antique business.

He stipulated, "That was before the great recession and the Greek government-debt crisis, or my folks would've had nothing to leave me."

I said, "I know that you're a bachelor, but have you ever considered marriage?"

"Way back, as a young man in New York, I dated plenty of women but never felt the urge to marry any. Later, I quit relationships altogether."

"Are you gay?"

He laughed and said, "I tried that too, but it didn't work out. In essence, I lack interest in sexual relationships."

I smiled and assured him, "This topic is off the record, if you wish."

His mannerism became extremely foreign as he said, "Leave it in, my dear, I'm not ashamed."

I then directed my questions to what was involved with owning an antique shop. I learned that Mr. A had equipped himself with loads of books and catalogues and talked with established antique dealers to learn what to look for before venturing into the enterprise. When asked where he found and purchased his treasures, his answer was, "Anywhere and everywhere. At auctions, antique shows, flea markets, estate sales, and occasionally even at other antique stores if the price is right."

He stressed that he needed to find bargains in order to sell at a profit.

To my question regarding age criteria for an antique, he replied, "Strictly speaking, everything 100 years or older is considered antique. That doesn't mean every object of that age is necessarily valuable. It depends how collectible a piece is."

I was going to ask how he could tell the real thing from the reproductions, when the front door chime went off as a couple entered the shop. "Excuse me for a moment," he said, and went to mind his customers.

Left alone, I took advantage to look around the small office niche. In contrast to the rest of Mr. A's shop, which was overstuffed with objects, his place of doing paperwork and research was bare and furnished to a minimum. There was a laptop and calculator on top of the desk; catalogues and volumes pertaining to art and antiques, neatly organized on small bookshelves; and a couple of file cabinets. That was it! I guessed that he did not want people to wander into his office looking for treasures.

He came back and said, "Where were we?"

I asked, "I'm curious, how do you know if an object is a true antique and not a fake?"

"I look for signs of wear and age along with marks and signatures. Pottery and porcelain marks are easily visible, whereas I have to find them with a magnifier on jewelry. Silver is identified by the word 'sterling' or the number 925."

He continued, "I do black light testing where applicable."

"What's a black light?"

"That's ultraviolet lighting, which helps to see what human eyes can't. For instance, both green Depression glass and Vaseline glass will glow under a black light because of the uranium oxide content in the glass. Ultraviolet lights can also be used to test for authenticity of art works, like oil paintings."

Then he said, "Now to furniture. If the piece has drawers, I'm in luck. It's easy to spot an antique by the drawers because joints were not machine-cut until around 1860. If it has only a few dovetail joints with pins narrower than the dovetails, then the joint was made by hand. Symmetry is a sign that a furniture was machine-made. On handmade pieces, the rungs, slats, spindles, rockers, et cetera, are not uniform. A real antique is seldom cut to perfection.

"The wood finish can also date the piece. The finish on furniture made before 1860 is mainly shellac. A varnish or lacquer finish is a sign that it was manufactured later. The type of wood is another indicator of age. Real early furniture, from the Middle Ages until the end of the 17th Century, is for the most part oak. After that, woods like walnut and mahogany became popular."

Mr. A was about to elaborate on identifying English and American furniture styles, but I stopped him and stated, "I think that's all the information I need and may not even use everything I jotted down."

Ready to leave his shop, I said, "I need to query this to an appropriate publication, which will take some time. I'll let you know where and when the column is published."

CHAPTER 35

In Huntington Beach, Fourth of July fireworks are launched from the end of the pier. Watching them with my friend Crystal had become a tradition. It had started four years earlier when I was trying to cheer her up as she recovered from a nasty divorce. We hadn't missed the annual event since. Crystal lived in Seal Beach, and as parking anywhere in downtown Huntington Beach throughout the festivities proved to be a big challenge, we opted for riding our bicycles down to the ocean. To avoid the biggest crowds, we chose to view the fireworks from Bolsa Chica State Beach, an easy ride from both our homes.

We usually skipped the morning parade and other daytime entertainment on Main Street and the pier, meeting in the early evening for a picnic dinner on the sand at Bolsa Chica. The year of my investigation into Jake Unger's death was no exception. We chain-locked the bikes to the stands near the restrooms and then were lucky to find an empty spot on the beach to spread our blanket. The area around us soon became jam-packed with people.

Like me, Crystal was also in her early thirties but that's where the similarities ended. She was a petite woman of about 5'3" and had the vitality of a whirlwind.

We unpacked our picnic meals and spread everything on the blanket. I provided the main course of mini baguettes, Havarti cheese, and sliced red bell peppers. Crystal brought bottled water and dark chocolate for dessert. We ate without talking, enjoying the modest but hearty food, did some people watching, and listened to the soothing, rhythmic sound of the waves.

I had seen Crystal only four days earlier, but we had yet to really talk. Grabbing a quick bite to eat and then rushing off to see the musical had not left much time for conversation. Now there was all the time in the world while waiting for the fireworks to begin. My friend, a real estate agent, went into details about the fantastic beach-front property she had sold a couple weeks earlier and that the commission would help keep her head above water for some time. When that subject was exhausted, she became animated and raved about her new boyfriend. According to Crystal, this man was the best human being ever born to this world.

"He's an orthodontist with a practice in your neighborhood," she said. And with an impish grin she added, "If we get serious and start a family, our kids will have the best smiles in town!"

As we relished a splendid sunset, shimmering between water and horizon, she asked, "So what's new with you?"

I did not tell her about my immersion into detective work for two reasons. First, for the moment I had deliberately erased the investigation from my mind, not wanting to think, let alone talk about it. And number two, I remembered that Brenda was a dental hygienist. Even though she was far from being a dentist or orthodontist and only cleaned teeth, there was a chance she knew people in the dental field in the Huntington Beach area. So in answer to Crystal's question I talked about Dad's mid-life crisis.

She said, "You're lucky that he does nothing worse than roam around the country on a motorcycle. A few years ago, my dad's crisis landed him in the hospital."

"What happened?"

"He went from one extreme sport to another and couldn't get enough danger under his belt. As if mountain biking, rock climbing, and rappelling, didn't offer enough thrill, he got into land kiting, better known as kite landboarding."

"I don't know anything about kite landboarding. How does it work?" I asked.

"It's similar to kitesurfing but of course it's on land. It involves a kite and the use of a landboard, which is an oversized skateboard with foot straps. You hold on to the kite handle, and off you go. Large open areas with constant wind are needed for the sport. Sandy beaches, early in the morning when there aren't any people about, are perfect. According to my dad, you get blown by the wind to incredible heights, giving you a feeling of flying."

She giggled and said, "He pretended to have wings once too often. A foot strap got loose during the landing, and he crashed one foot into the ground."

"Ouch!"

"He double-fractured his leg and foot but was lucky not to have suffered even worse injuries. Needless to say, that took care of his mid-life crisis."

The sun had disappeared from the horizon, leaving a deep red afterglow. I would have been content to admire the wonders of nature in silence, but my friend chattered on, "When I inquired about news, I meant news about you, not your dad. Are you back to dating?"

"Not by a long shot," I replied, "but I did get an offer to spend two weeks in Paris, France." And I explained that back in May, in order to write one of my columns, I had interviewed a scientist who'd won a trip for two to that city and asked me to join him.

When telling her that I was undecided whether to take him up on the offer, she said, "For sure you'll take him up on it! What's your problem?"

"Don't you think it odd that he's asking me, a complete stranger, to spend a vacation with him?"

"Don't be complicated, Tara! It's obvious that the man likes you. Is he cute?"

"He's not bad looking, but that's beside the point."

"So what are you waiting for? An invitation like that doesn't come your way every day. Go have your fling in Paris and when you're back, I want to hear all about it."

"You're impossible," I stated, making it clear that the subject was closed.

At nine o'clock, we were treated to a spectacular show of fireworks, well worth the long wait. Apart from the loud explosions, bangs, and whistles, the visual effects never failed to delight. The show ended with a finale of several firework combinations, going off in rapid succession.

With the breathtaking display in the night's sky having come to an end, we gathered our belongings. Following other folks leaving the beach and guided by the beam of our flashlight, we strode through the sand to where we had left our bikes. My friend and I parted on Pacific Coast Highway, riding home in opposite directions. With the bicycles' head-and-tail-lights, and the fluorescent glow of our jackets and shoes, we could easily be spotted by motorists.

CHAPTER 36

In the course of that first week in July, the time was ripe to evaluate everything I had learned and make some sense of it. I spent hours systematically going over every piece of information I had gathered.

While on the job, I was in the habit of taking meticulous notes when interviewing sources, making certain I had things right for writing each article. Why the heck hadn't I applied that practice to the investigation? I asked myself. As it stood, I had been more than lax with taking notes. I could have kicked myself for not having documented all conversations. The only notes I had kept were of the technical jargon pertaining to what I needed for the piece I wrote about Julien's discovery. And that was work-related, of course. I had also jotted down Brenda's version of the dispute with her brother-in-law about the Unger Huntington Beach property.

For everything else that was discussed during interviews and phone conversations, let alone my own observations, I now had to rely on my memory. Granted, I did credit myself with having an excellent memory, but the task of carefully going over in my mind's eye all that was said and done remained a tedious chore.

There was an object in Mr. A's antique shop that had triggered a recollection about something important I'd missed. For the life of me, I could no longer remember what the thing was. It would come to me eventually, I mused. As for now, I painstakingly re-lived every moment pertaining to the Unger investigation since April 14, starting with the man himself. And this time, I decided to document all my thoughts as I went along, so I created a file on my laptop.

Everyone I had talked to confirmed that Jake Unger had been a bright star in his profession. A couple of statements came to mind. Konrad König had called him a physicist of the highest caliber, and the words of his former roommate, Rob Cloud, popped into my head: "Jake was a brilliant physicist, simply brilliant. I haven't met anyone who comes close to his genius." So the man's brain had been way above average. Could that have had anything to do with why he was killed? There was Brenda, who had clearly not been impressed with her husband's brilliance. On the contrary, she seemed to have resented it and felt neglected.

In that same manner I mulled over all the bits and pieces of information I had collected from each person concerned. My document file had grown to over twenty pages by Friday evening, and I was busy adding the deliberation I'd had with Julien on Balboa Island. Then I reread the entire document, but it got me nowhere near solving the crime, if it was a crime. Disgusted with myself, I gave up and went to bed.

I had to use the bathroom in the middle of the night. In my semi sleep, I fumbled for the light switch on the nightstand lamp and saw Midnight's green eyes glowing in the dark, before he jumped off my bed the second he realized I was about to get up.

I remarked, "I wish I had your eyes. You can see fine with the light turned off." He ignored me and headed for the cat bed at the opposite side of the bedroom.

By the time I sat on the toilet it hit me, the *lamp!* It was that desk lamp, surrounded by old maps and vintage photos, I had seen in Mr. A's shop that reminded me of something. Seconds later, the significance of it also dawned on me. And yes, it mattered that Jake Unger was a genius! I had missed the essence of that fact.

I donned my robe, went to the living room, and opened my laptop. Then I studied the document I had created that week, concentrating on the very beginning of my investigation. An hour later, I felt certain that I had figured it all out and knew who the murderer was. But wait - - I corrected myself - - *that is physically impossible!*

I still believed that I had arrived at the correct conclusion and knew who had killed Jake Unger. The motive also made perfect sense. But my earlier brainstorm met with a major stumbling block I couldn't bypass. Disillusioned, I went back to bed but could not fall asleep again. The discovery I had made during that night would not leave me any peace.

CHAPTER 37

On the next day, Saturday July 7, I drove to Pasadena for another visit with Oma. I arrived at the retirement home in the late morning and signed myself in at the reception desk.

Oma's caregiver appeared in no time and said, "Your grandma has been remarkably lucid in the last few days, I am pleased to report. She even asked for you and also for someone named Rubeen. Do you know who that could be?"

I shook my head and she continued, "I'm afraid, though, that she's physically getting extremely frail. She needs to keep up her strength, but we have a hard time getting her to eat. She may subconsciously want to end her life."

That statement shocked me but didn't seem to bother the caregiver, and she cheerfully added, "You're just in time for lunch; maybe you can convince her to eat. Wait here, I'll get her."

As soon as she was out of sight, I remembered that Oma had nicknamed Mom "Rubin," the German word for the ruby gemstone. Mom's birthday was in July; the ruby was her birthstone. It was July and Oma was asking for

Mom. Could she possibly have made the connection and realized that her daughter's birthday was coming up? It was probably a coincidence. The caregiver had said that Oma was having coherent days lately, but I did not think that we could expect miracles at this point.

When I saw Oma, I was shaken. She leaned heavily on the caregiver when they walked toward me, and I noticed that she had lost even more weight in the two weeks since my last visit.

I embraced her, then gently took over and guided her to the nursing home's dining room, where a good many tenants had already gathered for lunch.

Oma made eye contact with me and said, "Let's give this place a try."

I didn't know if she thought we were at a restaurant or just pretended that we were, but the fact that she had spoken an entire sentence was amazing.

I said, "Yes, let's!"

We were served a hot turkey sandwich with gravy and red cabbage on the side. I cut everything into bite-size pieces and handed Oma a fork. Slowly but surely she ate some of her meal and drank milk from a straw. The food was good, and I cleaned off my own plate. There was custard for dessert and Oma ate it all. Then she looked at me and grinned from ear to ear.

"I'm proud of you," I said.

"Proud of you," she repeated.

"But you also need to eat when I'm not here." And I could tell that she was no longer listening, her attention span gone.

After lunch, I took her for a walk on the grounds, where we went through our established routine. We checked out the hummingbird feeder for action, stopped by the water fountain and listened to its rhythmic splashing sound, then strolled over to the flower garden, where Oma admired the sunflowers and then settled on her favorite bench under the Juniper tree.

I played a little game by asking, "Where's Tara?"

She pointed at me.

"And who's Rubin?"

She pointed at me again, and I said, "No, Rubin is your daughter and my mom."

This confused her and made her agitated. She shook her head several times and I knew that I had made her frustrated. She was close to tears.

I stroked her hand gently and said, "Never mind, it's not important. How about if we have our story time now?"

She relaxed and said, "Story."

I started with, "The other day, I told you that I was playing at being a private detective. Well, I'm still doing it, and now I know who the villain is, even though it looks like a physical impossibility."

I kept talking, telling her all about the discovery I had made the night before. In detail I laid my reasoning for being absolutely certain that I was on the right track before her. I also shared my frustration at not finding a way around my current dilemma. I talked non-stop for nearly half an hour. What my entire monologue amounted to was nothing short of thinking aloud.

As always, Oma seemed to enjoy listening to my voice and felt at ease in my company. Every so often I looked directly at her and saw her smiling. What difference did it make that she did not understand most of what I said?

My visits and storytelling brought some joy and diversion into her lonely life.

After I had nothing more to add about my investigation, I described the fireworks I had watched on the Fourth of July but could no longer hold her attention. She appeared to have reverted into a world of her own. I reached over and held her hand and we sat in silence for a while.

Abruptly she exclaimed, "Go back!"

"You want to go back inside?" I asked.

She grabbed my arm and repeated, "Go back."

I had the distinct feeling that she was trying to tell me something. I did not press the matter, knowing from past experiences that she would get frantic if she could not make herself understood. Instead, I chatted about whatever came to mind until she was ready to leave the garden.

On the drive home it came to me. "Go back!" I shouted out aloud, all of a sudden knowing what that meant. Dear old Oma, you still have your wise moments, I thought. And in addition, you grasped more of my story than I'd ever imagined and hit the nail right on its head.

CHAPTER 38

At this point in my exploration I knew the identity of the killer, the motive, the how, where, and when but could not prove any of it. There was no doubt in my mind that I'd figured it all out but going to the authorities with my discoveries was as yet out of the question. I had no concrete evidence.

How did it work in mystery novels? Ah yes, the protagonist provoked the guilty person to confess or resort to the drastic step of trying to silence his or her accuser. I was desperate enough to go in that direction. The trick was to form a good plan, which would take some effort and time. However, I needed to get some private matters out of the way first.

It had been over ten days since I had talked with Mom, so my call to her was overdue.

I asked, "Did you get any more postcards from Dad?"

"No," she replied, "but he called. Apparently he's freeloading at your Uncle Charles' house for a few days."

"So he's in Albuquerque. Does that mean he's on his way home?"

"I assume so, although he wasn't about to let me know where he's headed next."

I inquired, "How are you holding up?"

"I'm coping."

"So whom are you having an affair with, the grocery store guy or the dog walker?" I joked.

"Neither. I've decided to have my mid-life crisis by going on a spending spree. Your dad will be surprised to find a new dining room set, and an exquisite Persian rug when he gets home."

"I see. You're paying him back where it hurts." Then I said, "I went to see Oma yesterday."

"How is she?"

"Mentally, she had an extremely good day, but she's turned to skin and bone. The caregiver told me that she doesn't want to eat any longer."

"I'm so sorry."

I stated, "She confused me with you. You need to go see her before it's too late."

"I will."

"I mean it, Mom! Drive down soon or you'll regret it later."

Next, I called Julien and announced, "I've solved the crime and only need to iron out some details. When it's all over, I'm ready to take you up on your Paris trip offer, if it still stands, that is."

"Of course it stands. You won't regret your decision, we'll have tons of fun." And he asked, "Who is the murderer, by the way?"

"I'd rather tell you who did it, and how I came to that conclusion, in person."

"You're making me curious, that's for sure." And he said, "I've got some news of my own and am proud to tell you that I've found the perfect rental for my lab, which I'm in the process of outfitting. Want me to show you the place?"

"I'd love to see it," I said.

"How about tomorrow?"

"Sorry, I'm working toward a deadline. It will have to be later in the week."

We settled on Thursday afternoon, July 12.

CHAPTER 39

Driving to Long Beach along Pacific Coast Highway took me only twenty minutes, and the GPS's automated female voice guided me to the correct address. I drove into the underground parking structure below the two-story office building that housed Julien's lab and found a spot designated for visitors. The elevator took me up to the ground floor where I studied the ledger. In suites 101, 102, and 103 an architectural bureau, a chiropractor, and an accountant were listed on that level. The second floor was registered with the suite number 201 only, with no business name written next to it.

I suddenly remembered that Julien had mentioned that his new lab was on the top floor, so I got back into the elevator and went up another flight, where he came to greet me at his threshold.

"Come on in," he beamed, "I'll show you around. The building is brand new, and I was lucky to snatch the entire second level all to myself. My name isn't even listed on the ledger yet." Full of enthusiasm he continued, "And what's more, the place is only about thirty minutes in walking distance from my apartment, so I'll get some exercise anytime I feel like it."

We first entered the office area. The desk held a computer with two large monitors and a printer. A huge whiteboard was fastened to the outer wall, which I assumed was for mathematical configurations. The door to the lab was wide open and he guided me through it.

My first impression was that of a vast space with a high, sloped ceiling, allowing natural indirect light in. On second glance, I noticed that the large room was sparingly furnished, mostly with technical equipment, which I had no way of identifying. There was also a refrigerator, a freezer, and a large sink.

Julien said, "This place is perfect for laboratory use. It has chemically-resistant covered flooring and all the utilities are located in a space above the ceiling. There aren't any wet chemicals or other hazards in here yet, but I was assured that the ventilation system is superb."

He went on, "I've moved some of my old equipment in but the majority is new and the most up-to-date available on the market. Many of the larger apparatuses I've ordered have yet to be delivered; that's why the room looks half empty. Once it's ready, it'll be a state-of-the-art research lab."

He took me on a show-and-tell walk around the vast room. There was a Ballistic Galvanometer setup, and he explained that it was used for estimating the quantity of charge flow running through it. The Newton's Ring apparatus confirmed the wave theory of light. I learned that a sonometer was a device used for studying transverse vibrations of a string.

We got to a long, rigid surface with a linear scale attached, accommodating holders for lenses and screens. I asked, "What's that called?"

"That's an optical bench," he replied, "used for laser-and-optics-related experiments."

There was an Ultrasonic Measurement Lab he pointed out, which was for studying various parameters of ultrasonic waves. The coupled oscillators were connected in such a way that energy could be transferred between them.

By the time he showed me the interferometer tool, I was getting tired of asking what the thing was good for and just nodded.

"And that's a traveling microscope," he declared.

"Oh, it travels," I remarked with a smirk.

"Exactly! It's mounted in a manner that allows it to be moved along its base."

There was a transparent, rectangular container with built-in special gloves sitting on a workbench. I pointed to it and said, "I know what that is and what it's for. I think the thing's called a glovebox."

"Correct."

A high-speed centrifuge was resting on a counter against a wall. Above it, I noticed shelves with racks containing empty tubes and bottles. An incubator also stood along the same wall.

As the tour of the large space came to an end, I said, "Your new lab is impressive!"

"It will be, once the larger equipment is delivered and in place. I can hardly wait to put it all to good use."

Then he said, "Let's go back to the office and check the calendar. We have to decide on a date for the Paris trip. But first, you've got to tell me about the discovery you made in your investigation."

"You bet," I said and followed him out of the lab.

CHAPTER 40

We sat down in Julien's office, he in his swivel desk chair, and I in a comfortable armchair, and he said, "I can't offer you anything but water to drink."

"I'm fine," I assured him.

"Don't keep me in suspense any longer," he begged.

I said, "It's a long story, but I'll try to make it brief. Ever since we had our walk around Balboa Island, I mulled over every talk I'd had with each person, but it didn't get me any closer in solving the crime. The other day, I paid my neighbor a visit at his antique shop - - that's a story on its own, but I won't bore you with it. The reason I bring it up is because, amid all other clutter of antiques, I noticed an item that rang a bell concerning my investigation. But, for the life of me, I couldn't later remember what the object was.

"Then, in the middle of the night, I woke up and did remember. From that point on, everything fell into place and became crystal clear. I should have figured it out much earlier. After all, Dr. Jake Unger was considered a genius."

I took a deep breath and said, "It was a lamp!"

Julien gave me a blank look and said, "What about a lamp?"

"The lamp in my neighbor's antique shop reminded me of the heat lamp in Jake Unger's lab."

"I still don't get it," he said.

"Let me backtrack. When I said a moment ago that I mulled over every talk I'd had with everyone concerned, I didn't just mean the people I interviewed about the murder case. I also scrutinized the conversations you and I had."

"And?"

I stated, "When I first had my suspicion that Jake Unger might have been murdered and called you, asking for Rob Cloud's last name, you made a statement that should have put me on the right track immediately, but I didn't see the significance of what you said. You remarked that you sympathized with me for being gung-ho on detecting, but you pointed out that the explosion may have been nothing more than an accident. You stated that Jake may have been absent-minded by placing the ammonium nitrate by the heat lamp."

I continued, "And stupid me, I didn't make the connection again during lunch in the Mexican restaurant in Balboa. At the time I was beating myself up, saying that I might be wrong and that the explosion may have been an accident after all. You agreed on that possibility and then repeated more or less the same thing about the ammonium nitrate being too close to the heat lamp."

"I remember all that, but I don't get what your big breakthrough is," he said.

"Julien! How did you know that the ammonium nitrate caused the explosion and that there even was a heat lamp in Jake's lab? You claimed that you didn't go into the lab."

He stared at me and said, "It was stated in the fire investigator's report."

"Who gave you details of the report?"

"You did."

"No, Julien. I told you that according to the fire investigator's report, the explosion was accidental due to careless handling of a flammable substance. I never went into other details about the report, nor did I mention what that substance was, and I certainly never brought up the heat lamp."

I looked him in the eye and said, "The game is up. You instigated that explosion and killed your friend and colleague for five million dollars."

"You're out of your mind!" he shouted.

I went on, "On that night, when all the puzzle pieces fell into place, I also recalled something else. It was a minor thing, really, but it fit. The day I interviewed you for my column out at Ruby's, you gave me the strangest look when I told you about the appointment I had in the late afternoon to view Jake Unger's lab. At the time I was unsure of the expression on your face, but now I know. It was fear."

"Fear of what?" he said, with a scornful look.

"That I could have seen you coming out of the Ungers' guesthouse in the late afternoon."

"You're fantasizing. I went to see Jake in the morning. Remember?"

"That's true, you did. That was the one stumbling block I had to overcome. And it was my grandmother who got me to see how simple the solution was. You went back to the Unger residence at 3:30. I'm sure you recall what I suggested about Brenda during our consultation, namely, that a surprise attack would have worked in her case, and that she looked through the window to check what Jake was doing. Well, that's exactly what happened, except that it was you, not Brenda.

"You stood between the garage and the guesthouse, peeked into his lab through the side window, making sure he was concentrating on a project with his back to the door. Then you went inside and knocked him unconscious. With Jake rendered powerless, it was easy as pie to set things up for the explosion. You were the last person paying your friend a visit. In other words, you are our notorious X."

Julien tried to look amused and said, "This is all fabrication, but I'm going to humor you and play along. What motive could I possibly have had to kill Jake?"

"As I mentioned before, five million is a good reason to kill if one has an evil streak. You stole his entry to the contest and sent it to Tops & Associates as your own."

"That's absurd. He was still working on his version, and I had mine all finished and ready to go."

"I bet it was the other way around. And that is why you needed to destroy all the evidence by blowing his lab to pieces. Dr. Jake Unger was the real genius, not you!"

Angry now, he said, "You can't prove any of this."

"I'm willing to try," I said. "For starters, I think it won't be too hard to find out the exact date you submitted your entry to the contest. I have a hunch you just made the deadline. Another thing would be to locate Jake Unger's copy of his data. I understand he was a meticulous fellow and would have kept remote records."

Julien said, "You have no evidence that puts me at the crime scene at 3:30 that afternoon. The neighbor you told me about cannot identify the person he saw looking through Jake's lab window, and you also said that he had no view to the guesthouse entrance."

"Oh, but you're wrong. There is another witness. I can't tell you who the person is for his or her protection."

"You're bluffing," he said, but I could tell that he was getting scared.

There was an uncomfortable silence, and I sensed that he was making up his mind about how to handle me. I was well aware of the danger I had put myself in. The vibes coming off this man were no longer pleasant. I felt for the Mace in my purse, making sure that it was there, while telling myself: Act in total control, Tara. Don't show any kind of weakness.

He seemed to change tactic, however, and asked, "Does that mean you're not coming to Paris with me?"

I countered, "Did you plan all along that, once in Paris, you'd hit me over the head and toss me into the Seine when no one would be watching, in case I stumbled onto the truth?"

"That's insulting! I invited you on the trip before I even knew about your detective hobby. Remember? The reason I asked you along was because I liked you. I still do, as a matter of fact. And now that you've become feisty and turned into a challenge, I appreciate you even more!"

He made an attempt at a grin and said, "I'll get us some water from the fridge and then I'll tell my side of the story. Once you know it all, I'm positive we can reach some kind of an agreement."

The audacity of the man made me wince inside, but outwardly, I kept my cool. Showing my true feeling at this point would be a mistake.

CHAPTER 41

Julien came back with two small water bottles and said, "You're not wired, are you? If so, I have instruments here that can detect such a device."

"Recording you hadn't occurred to me," I said.

"It never hurts to make sure. Let me have a look at your smartphone."

I handed it over. He made certain that it was not in video mode and then gave it back with a bow. It struck me that the man, despite the predicament he found himself in, hadn't lost his charm. His demeanor bordered on the theatrical. In the past, this might have amused me but now it was a huge turnoff.

He went into his spiel with, "Let me start at the beginning. You're right, Jake was a genius and had a few scientific breakthroughs under his belt. Yet he had an aversion to sharing his wisdom with other physicists. Already back when we worked together in the government-funded lab, he was secretive and kept his discoveries to himself whenever possible. When forced to work as a team, he was impossible to get along with. As we both became self-employed, Jake soon made a name for himself in the field.

Elite companies solicited him as a contractor, while I had to hustle to make a living as an independent physicist."

I realized that he needed to get more off his chest before he was ready to confess to the murder and listened quietly as he went on, "And then Tops & Associates sponsored the contest. That was my chance to get ahead. It wasn't so much the money but the prestige that was the big draw for me. Winning that contest not only would guarantee a nice chunk of research cash, but the notability would set me up for life.

"In between consulting contracts, I worked hard on coming up with a solution for the contest. Finding an eco-friendly cellulose-derived product that was going to replace petroleum-based packaging was not an easy task. Believe me, I did the math and tried all sorts of experiments, but in the end, nothing held up. I wasted an entire year on it, spending money and time. In February, I came close but lacked one lousy element. I admit, winning that contest became an obsession with me. The deadline for the entry was April, 21. The closer I got to it the more frantic I became."

I nodded as he picked up his tale again, saying, "I knew that Jake was also a contestant. Toward the end of March I called him, trying to feel him out. It came as no surprise that he parted with no data of his, but he did say that he had a solution and was in the process of smoothing out a couple of minor kinks. I told him part of my version, hoping he would confirm that I was on the right track. He stated in his usual matter of fact way, 'You're not even close.' He didn't have the decency to tell me where I went wrong. On the contrary, he refused to discuss the matter further and we ended the call."

His eyes burned into mine as he said, "You can't imagine how desperate I was on that Saturday, a week before the deadline. I decided to make one last appeal in person and went to see him that morning. Don't get me wrong, I didn't expect him to divulge his own solution. I just wanted him to point me in the right direction concerning my own calculations, which I was sure he could help me with.

"Like I already mentioned, he closed the door to his lab and we stayed in the other room of the guesthouse. But what I hadn't told you is that we got into a major fight. I first asked him how far along he was with the contest project, to which he answered that he had it all ready to go and would submit it on Monday, prototype and all. When I asked for guidance with my own version, he wouldn't even listen to what I'd come up with. Instead, he told me that I'd always been too lazy to figure things out for myself.

"That got me hopping mad. I may have my faults but laziness isn't one of them. So I threw all sorts of angry words at him, including that he was a stubborn, self-centered son-of-a-bitch. Typical of Jake, he never lost his cool and told me to leave in his calm, rational way. I stormed out of there, seeing red."

He took a few large gulps of water and then revealed, "I drove home, thinking, I'll win that contest and Jake will be my enabler, whether he likes it or not. I sulked for hours and then made up my mind to drive back to Huntington Beach and try again. Equipped with a reflex hammer in my trouser pocket, I left my apartment in mid-afternoon and - - -"

I interrupted, "Is that the small hammer doctors use to check one's knees for reflexes?"

"Yes," he stated, "but mine is heavy duty. I use it in a science experiment I call the hammer gravity trick. It's still in my apartment; I'll show you the trick someday."

I could not believe his arrogance. The man still thought we'd stay in contact after all was said and done! Inwardly, I was repulsed but worked hard at not showing it.

I said, "And you wore a baseball cap so you wouldn't be recognized by any potential witnesses."

"The hat was an afterthought. I was ready to leave my apartment when I went back to get it. I didn't wear it because of any potential witnesses, though, like you assume, since at that time I had no intention of any wrongdoing. I wanted to avoid being recognized by Brenda. She's the type of person who would question my coming back, and I didn't want to deal with her."

He resumed his monologue, "Where was I? Oh yeah, I went back to see Jake. By the way, I didn't plan to hit him with the hammer. The idea was to threaten and pressure him, if all else failed. I also had no intention to blow up his lab when I left home. Those decisions came at the spur of the moment as I seized the opportunity. On my drive over from Long Beach to Huntington Beach, I rehearsed what I intended to say to Jake. I even made a detour and drove around Seal Beach for a while, until I had it down pat. First, I planned to apologize for my earlier conduct and then charm him into helping me with my project.

"That all fell apart when I came face to face with him. Like I said, I didn't want to have to deal with Brenda again, so I bypassed their main house and went straight to the guesthouse. It's true, I did indeed first go along the outside of it and looked through the lab window, making sure Jake was there. He was busy typing on his desktop computer. I knew from that morning's experience that he didn't lock the guesthouse door, so I walked to the front and let myself in."

Julien avoided looking at me but stared at the wall over my shoulder, and I supposed he re-lived the scene once more as he continued, "I sidestepped the first room and found the door to his lab wide open. He must have heard me and turned his head. 'You again,' he said, and got to his feet. Then he pointed at the door and ordered, 'Get out!' I started on my rehearsed speech, but he wouldn't listen and yelled, 'Out!' directing his outstretched arm toward the door.

"An overwhelming rage came over me, and I stepped closer, pulling the hammer out of my pants pocket. Only threatening him with the thing was no longer an option. I swung it high, then watched it come crashing down over his head. In the split second before the hammer hit his skull, Jake reached for a flash drive that had sat on his desk. Then he crumbled to the floor in slow motion. For a brief moment I was stunned by what I'd done. Then the perfect opportunity came to mind, and I jumped into action before Jake had a chance to regain consciousness."

There was a cockiness in his demeanor as he went on, "I grabbed the flash drive out of his hand and inserted it into his computer. Just as I had expected, the entire documentation for the contest entry was all there: the listing of chemicals used and their quantities - including the calculation of the reactants' theoretical yield, detailed procedures, observations, and product analysis - from the theoretical down to the actual yield. There was also a large yellow envelope marked 'contest factual' and the prototype of the finished product sitting on Jake's desk. I checked the content of the envelope and found the printed version of his documentation headed by a cover letter. I was in awe of the find. Jake's entire entry to the contest lay before me! It was complete and ready to be sent off. All I had to do was take it, copy and change it to my own name, and submit it.

"Then I looked around the lab. It was obvious that Jake had also been in the process of working on a different project. I saw the ammonium nitrate and also noticed the heat lamp sitting on a workbench clear across the room."

I butt in, "What exactly is ammonium nitrate and what does it do again?"

"It's a chemical compound and can be found as a natural mineral in the Atacama Desert in Chile, but what is now used is strictly synthetic. As to what it does: left alone, not much, but put it next to a heating device, and you've got yourself a nice explosion and fire."

He continued, "It stands to reason that I needed to destroy the lab with everything in it, including Jake. I was certain that he had all his findings in a document file on his hard drive and also another copy somewhere else in the room. Discovering that ammonium nitrate was a piece of luck. In order to be safe, that particular chemical needs to be in a cool, well-ventilated area and it is important to store it in a tightly closed container.

"I went across the room and turned on the heat lamp, then opened up the vessel containing the ammonium nitrate and placed it right by the heating device. I didn't know how long it would take but was sure that, given its close exposure to heat, the thing would explode soon and set the entire lab on fire. I checked my watch. It was 3:50. Jake was still out cold and bleeding from the gash on his head. I kept my fingers crossed that he'd stay that way for several minutes longer. I left the place with the hammer in one trouser pocket, the flash drive and prototype in the other, and the yellow envelope tucked under my shirt.

"On the drive home I thought, if anyone saw and recognized me either going in or coming out of the guesthouse, I'd state that I paid my colleague another friendly visit. It was a bit of a gamble that Jake might regain consciousness and make his way out of there before the lab would blow up. Since that was out of my control, I didn't dwell on it. As for the wound on his head, I hoped that it would be blamed on debris falling on him caused by the explosion."

He gave me a crooked smile and said, "I take it that was exactly the way it went down."

With that, his confession came to an end. There was complete silence between us for several moments. During his entire admission I was thinking, he's not going to let me out of here alive. I had better be prepared. For his part, he seemed to have re-lived the whole ghastly deed all over again, a faraway look was in his eyes.

In another instant the spell was gone and he said in his natural, charming way, "So you see, Tara, I had no other way to win the contest."

"But there were many more entries from other scientists, and you couldn't know in advance who'd win," I said.

"Ah, you're wrong. I knew for certain that Jake's discovery would be the winner, especially after I looked at the documentation on the flash drive. His version was a masterpiece. It met with all the required criteria and was cost-efficient to boot. No one could surpass it."

I kept quiet and he said, "As I mentioned before, you have no evidence. If you went to the police it would be your word against mine, and I guarantee you that it'll never come to a trial. Nobody would believe your wild story. They'll just say you made it up for the headline. Be reasonable! What was Jake Unger to you anyway, other than a complete stranger whom you met once? Be smart and forget the whole thing. I'll make it up to you!"

He reached over and, holding my hand while staring at me, said, "Your eyes are green right now like a cat's."

It took all my willpower not to shudder in disgust and withdraw my hand as he said, "By the way, my offer about the Paris trip still stands."

I was stunned and could not believe his arrogance. But maybe this gave me a chance to leave his laboratory alive.

I stammered, "I'll think about it."

"You do that. And as I said, if you're smart, the two of us can come to an agreement. Think on that too!"

CHAPTER 42

While driving home, I had no illusion that I was out of danger. I had been prepared to spray him with Mace and kick him in the nuts, if necessary. That he let me leave his lab without a hitch came as a welcome surprise. On the downside, now I had no idea when and how the attack would come. That it would come, I knew with certainty. On that day, he'd been bowled over by my sudden accusation of his crime and ill-equipped to deal with me. That would change as soon as he took the time to form a plan and had the opportunity to act on it.

The idea that he still planned to spend two weeks in Paris with me was ludicrous. Or could he be so damned sure of himself to believe I was no threat to him? Fat chance! The man was smart. He had a doctorate in physics, no less, and I guessed a certain amount of street smarts too.

In case this was not clear, I want to tell the reader right here and now that I had never intended to join Julien on the trip. Telling him of my decision to accept his invitation was to throw him off his guard. Since I'm on the subject of venting my thoughts and feelings, I also want to be completely honest. Before I had figured out that Julien was the killer, his tremendous charm was not lost on me.

I'd had a strong physical attraction to the guy, no doubt, but fought it off. As I told him in Oma's words, "*Gebrannte Kinder fürchten das Feuer.*" A good thing that I had kept my head above water this time, so my knack for getting into relationships with the wrong kind of men did not include a murderer.

I mulled over the tense exchange we'd had in the office at Julien's new lab, ending with his confession. Telling him that there was another witness besides the Ungers' next door neighbor was a complete fabrication, but I thought it left him with a bit of worry. And he was correct that I had no evidence of his crime, nor could I deny that it came down to his word against mine.

What did this evil man mean by stating, "I'll make it up to you?" And what did he have in mind about an agreement? Was it an attempt at bribing me with a million or two? You've got some nerve, Dr. Julien Floyd, assuming you could buy me off, and no clue at all as to what makes me tick.

When I pulled into my parking space at the apartment building, I realized that I found myself in the same predicament as at the very beginning of my investigation: I could not take my findings to the authorities.

CHAPTER 43

For the rest of the day and evening I documented all the information I had gathered, including Julien's long account and confession, entering every little detail. While printing the pages out, I made the resolution that it was time to confide in someone. Not wanting to drag any outsider into the mess I had created left me few choices as to who that person could be.

It was already past nine o'clock at night when I called Brenda, using my cellphone rather than the landline.

She didn't pick up and when voicemail took over I stated, "This is Tara Blunt. I have important news. Please call me back at - - -"

Brenda came on the line before I had a chance to give her my smartphone number. She said, "So what's this important news that can't wait until tomorrow morning?"

I first apologized for calling at that late hour and then said, "I know who the killer is and would like to tell you about it in person. Is there a chance that you could see me tomorrow?"

I must have shocked her. She took a few seconds before she said, "Really? You know for sure who did it?"

I said, "So far I have no proof but I'm 100% positive that I know who set off the explosion and murdered your husband. I even have an admission from the killer."

"Who is it?"

"I'm not calling from my landline, but I'd rather not reveal the person's name over the phone. So when can I see you tomorrow?"

"I get off work at 2:30 and then pick Logan up at his preschool's daycare. I'll get home between 3:00 and 3:10, depending on traffic."

"I'll come to your house then," I said and ended the call.

Later in bed with Midnight at my feet, I said to him, "From here on out I have to be on my guard. Most important, I'll make sure no one's following me, wherever I go."

He just purred, having not a worry in the world.

CHAPTER 44

When I arrived at the Unger bungalow, Brenda steered me to the kitchen, where she was in the process of preparing a snack for Logan.

She said, "Let me get him settled first, and then we can go sit in the living room."

She spread soft cheese onto a couple of crackers, cut a few grapes in half, and then sat the small plate of finger food plus a sippy cup of chocolate milk in front of him, where he had been patiently waiting in his booster chair at the kitchen table.

I smiled at the well-behaved toddler and said, "That looks delicious."

"Delicious," he repeated, and then concentrated on eating.

Brenda turned to me and asked, "Can I get you anything to eat or drink?"

"No, thanks," I said.

Minutes later, with Logan off to play with his toys in the next room, Brenda and I got comfortable in the living room.

She blurted, "Tell me already who it is! I can't take the suspense much longer."

I replied, "Before I do, it is only fair that I warn you. Since the killer unmasked himself to me, I am in danger. As far as he's concerned, I know it all and need to be silenced. By disclosing the person's name, I'll put you at risk too."

"Don't worry about me. I'm not scared," she stated.

"Think about Logan. What would happen to him without you?"

That made her hesitate for a moment. Then she brushed it off and said, "I can take precautions. Besides, the person won't know that I know." She begged, "Tell me already, who murdered Jake and blew up his lab?"

And so I did, going into the entire morbid story from A to Z. She listened carefully, without ever interrupting.

As I came to the end she exploded, "The wicked bastard! And all for winning the lousy contest."

I took a large envelope out of my bag and, handing it to her, said, "It's all documented in those pages. Put the envelope in a safe place. If something happens to me, give it to the police."

"Go to them now," she said, "you have his confession."

"He gave it orally, and I'm sure if questioned by the authorities, he'd deny it all and claim that I made the whole thing up."

"So what are you going to do?"

"I need to find solid evidence. For starters, did you happen to see Julien go over to the guesthouse a second time? That would have been around 3:30, just a few minutes before you left to run errands?"

"No. I only saw him come by in the morning and not in the afternoon."

"That would have made it too easy for me," I said. "Do you know if your husband used a remote backup server for the data on his computer? If so, are you aware what outfit he used?"

"Sorry, I don't know. I'm ashamed to say that I wasn't much interested in what he did. And if he kept records about such a server they'd have gone up in smoke with the rest of his lab."

"I was afraid of that." And I asked, "Who took care of paying the bills?"

She replied, "We had a joint checking account for household stuff where we each wrote checks. Jake had a separate account for his use alone. Anything that had to do with his work and research he paid from his own account."

"Do me a favor. If you receive any strange invoices within the next two months, let me know."

I couldn't think of anything else to say and was ready to leave. Still clutching the big envelope to herself she asked, "May I read what's in here once I'm by myself?"

"Sure, but it's basically the same thing I've told you. I'm giving it to you for safekeeping in case something happens to me."

A lone tear rolled down her cheek as she said, "We didn't have much in common and grew apart, but Jake was the father of my son and I loved him once. He didn't deserve to die such a brutal death. Curse that bastard, Julien Floyd!"

I hadn't noticed Logan coming into the living room until he repeated, "Curse that bastard."

Once I arrived at the front door of my apartment, I carefully turned the key in the lock, then slowly pushed the door open a quarter of an inch. The tiny piece of paper I had placed between the door and the frame as I left home earlier fell to the ground. With a relieved sigh I stepped inside.

CHAPTER 45

I was sneaking by Mr. A's door on Saturday morning, July 14, when he flung it open and stood in his robe, proclaiming, "Good morning, Tara! Already going out for your neighborhood stroll?"

"Right, but instead of staying in the area, I've decided to walk around Main Street and the pier." And I added, "I'll get to writing up the column about your shop soon."

"Looking forward to reading it!" he yelled after me as I moved on.

At my car, I did a bit of inspecting. I had taken a few precautions when parking it the day before. As with my apartment door, I had done the little paper trick on my Honda too. I first opened the driver-side door and let the little scrap of paper fall down to the ground. Then the same happened when I did likewise with the trunk lid. The hood also proved untampered with. I opened its lid and checked under the hood.

I'm no mechanic by any means, but after coming home from Brenda's house the day before, I had scrutinized the entire layout under the hood and taken a picture. I now compared what I saw with the photo on my smartphone. If something would have been amiss or disconnected, I'm sure I'd have noticed. Next, I crouched on my hands and knees and inspected the bottom of the car. I did not detect any kind of device attached to it. Finally, I decided that it was safe to take the car for a spin.

On the drive to Main Street, I frequently checked my rearview mirror, making sure I was not followed. I had not been down to the pier in a while and was looking forward to it, but I had a more important reason for choosing downtown Huntington Beach for my walk that day. The area was never deserted. No matter what time of day or night, plenty of tourists and locals gathered there, especially in the summer.

I parked at my usual spot on a cross street and then walked briskly down Main, being alert to people around me. When I got to the pier, the fog was lifting and it was becoming a pleasant warm day. I stopped to watch the early-morning surfers and could not help but be reminded of the last time I had stood in the same spot, observing them. That had been on the day I met Julien to interview him concerning his discovery that had won him the contest. *His* discovery and *his* winning the contest. What a farce!

That had only been six weeks ago, I thought, but it felt like six years. Soon afterward, I started to have serious doubts about the explosion having been accidental. At the time I had told myself more than once, let it go, Tara. It's not your problem. Now, watching the surfers from the pier high above, I questioned my involvement. Did I regret meddling and consequently having put my life at risk? Yes, to a degree. On the other hand, I knew good and well that I'd have lost all self-respect if I had let a killer go free.

I continued my walk to the end of the pier. Behind Ruby's diner, I watched a fisherman reeling in a catch. Once he had it out of the ocean and dangling from the line, I saw that it was a ten-inch bonito. He dropped it into a large bucket filled with water. Glancing into the bucket, I noticed that he'd already caught two smaller fish earlier.

I said, "I know what you're having for dinner tonight." To which he replied, "I need to catch a few more, we're a family of six."

On my way back, while happening upon a pelican sitting on the pier railing, I thought, you have an uncomplicated life. As long as there's fish in the ocean you can dive for, your belly is full and you're satisfied. At this point in my life, I wished that all I had to worry about was where my next meal would come from. As if the big bird had taken offense to my thoughts, he stretched his wings wide and flew off.

For the umpteenth time since getting up that day, I did some somber reflecting on how I could find tangible evidence of Julien's crimes. By the time I had reached my Honda, I'd thought of a few possibilities, only to reject each one.

CHAPTER 46

As soon as I turned onto my street, I saw the commotion. There was no point in trying to pull into my building's parking area, as it was blocked off by fire engines and police vehicles. Yellow crime tape stretched across the width of the street from sidewalk to sidewalk. A police officer motioned me to turn around. I felt my heart beating faster as I made a U-turn and parked on the next cross street. Then I ran back toward my apartment building and came to a halt before the crime tape, where a crowd of my neighbors stood in an uproar, all talking at once.

I noticed Mr. A among the spectators and was about to go over and ask him what had happened, when two officers, with a handcuffed person between them, marched out of the apartment complex. As the trio walked toward a parked police car, they passed by about eight yards from where I stood, and I saw that the handcuffed man was Julien. He spotted me and stood still for a second, making his escorts also stop in their tracks.

He made eye contact and said, "You win, Tara." And there was pure evil in his glance as he added, "I should have gotten rid of you right away."

I watched as one of the police officers helped Julien into the back of the police vehicle, making sure he didn't bump his head. Then they drove off with their charge.

I hurried over to Mr. A and asked, "What is going on? Why are all these people gathered out here?" And even as I formed the question, I had already guessed the answer.

He replied, "Everyone in the building had orders to get out until the bomb is inactivated."

"A bomb!" I shouted. "Where?" But I knew the answer to that too.

"In your apartment, but don't worry, the bomb squad is working on it as we speak."

"No!" I screamed, jumped over the crime tape and ran toward the apartments' entrance, before he had finished his sentence.

A police officer ordered, "Stop! You're not allowed into the building!" I ignored him and kept running. He caught up and forcefully detained me.

I tried to get away and yelled, "I'm the tenant of apartment B2, where there's a bomb. My cat is inside the apartment!"

He still had a hard grip on me but said in a friendly tone, "You need to calm down, Miss. Experts are in your apartment, neutralizing the explosive device. You can go in as soon as it's safe to do so. In the meantime, let's go back to the sidewalk," and he escorted me to the pavement.

I cried tears of frustration and fear for Midnight as I stood amid my fellow neighbors once more but was left with no choice other than to wait it out like everyone else. I prayed, "Dear God, let Midnight be okay."

Then the image of handcuffed Julien, giving me the evil eye, came to mind. He had obviously seized the opportunity, knowing my routine of taking early morning walks. I had told him so myself! And my next thought was that he had wasted no time and must have worked on creating that bomb the minute I'd left his lab the other day.

Eventually, I was permitted into my apartment and found Midnight hiding under my bed, scared but unharmed. As expected, my big black feline had been petrified of the strangers roaming around his domain.

Two police officers had accompanied me in, and after I made sure that Midnight was fine, they inquired into my personal data and had tons of questions, noting the info on their report. I had a few questions of my own and learned that Mr. A had called 911 to report suspicious activities in the apartment above his. When the department dispatched a couple of their law enforcers to check up on apartment B2, they had caught Julien in the act. He had been in the process of screwing the grill back onto the air conditioning vent.

I said, "You mean he placed a bomb into the AC?"

"Exactly," one of the officers replied. "The explosive device would have been triggered as soon as you'd have turned the air-conditioning system on. You are lucky that Mr. Apostolos notified us of the intruder and we caught him red-handed."

All of a sudden I felt stifling hot. Whether this was because I had had a near miss with death or that the outside temperature was rising to above 80 degrees on that summer day was unclear. I asked, "Is it okay to turn the air on now?"

The officer who had so far done all the talking assured me, "The special bomb unit people took care of it; there's nothing to worry about any longer." And he set the thermostat switch to 'cool'.

My next question was, "I assume he picked the lock to get in?"

"No doubt. It was relatively easy to pick. You should get yourself more secure double locks."

That same officer, who was obviously in charge, said, "And now, we have a few more things to ask you, Ms. Blunt. First off, do you know a person by the name of Julien Floyd?"

"I sure do," I replied.

"Do you have any idea why he would want to blow up your apartment and what reason he could have for wanting you dead?"

"I know why, and it has nothing to do with terrorism." And I asked, "Do you have a couple hours? It's a long story."

I got as far as the explosion in Dr. Jake Unger's lab with my statement, when the officer interrupted and said, "Looks like this involves more than one felony. We would like you to come to the police station and give your full account to our detectives." And so I did.

As I drove home hours later, I thought, funny how things turned out. When Julien set up that explosive device in my apartment and was caught in the act by the police, he himself provided that tangible evidence I had been seeking.

CHAPTER 47

On that same evening, I took Mr. A out for dinner to a fancy restaurant. We both ordered prime rib and complemented the meal with a good Petite Sirah wine. We ate in agreeable silence. Mr. A seemed to savor every bite, and I satiated my hunger. All the anxiety and stress of the day had made me famished.

It wasn't until the end of the meal and over coffee that we started our discussion. He said, "That was excellent! Thank you so much." And his mannerism became extremely foreign as he continued, "But your invitation was not de rigueur, my dear Tara."

"It's the least I can do. You saved my life, Mr. A!" And I pleaded, "Tell me everything about this morning, down to the last detail."

"It was really simple," he said. "Remember, I stood at my door as you left for a walk, and you told me that you'd take the car for a change?" He did not expect an answer to his question and went on, "As I came out of my bathroom after showering a while later, I heard someone go upstairs. I first assumed that it was you who had come back sooner than expected. But then I looked out my back window and noticed that your Honda was not parked in its assigned spot. I quickly threw on some clothes and climbed up the flight of stairs.

"I stood in front of your closed door and listened with my ear to it. There was definitely someone inside your apartment fumbling around. I thought it was a burglar and hightailed it back down to my place, where I called the authorities. I told them that there was a robber in apartment B2, the one directly above mine. They came pretty fast, within ten minutes or so, and without sirens blaring. I appreciated that fact, since I thought that there was a burglary in progress. Two police officers walked by my open door, and without saying a word I pointed upstairs, so that the person I thought was a thief wouldn't get forewarned. As it turned out, the guy did much worse than stealing and was caught just in time."

He sighed and said, "But you know that, of course. Getting back to my story, soon after the officers went up to your apartment all hell broke loose. Now there were sirens galore, and a loudspeaker blared from one of their vehicles, ordering everyone to evacuate the building. You showed up some ten minutes or so afterwards. I confess, until you tried to get inside, I had totally forgotten about Midnight. But even if I'd remembered, it's doubtful that I'd have been able to coax him out."

He shrugged and said, "I had planned to attend an auction today, but with all that uproar in our building and whatnot, I was too late. When the two police officers escorted you to your apartment after it was safe to go inside, another one came to my place, and I had to give a statement. And anyway, I had lost the desire for business as usual."

Then he smiled and requested, "Now it's your turn to tell me all about that villain of yours who tried to kill you."

So for the second time that day, I told it all. At the police station I did so out of necessity, but now I delivered the sordid facts as a token of my gratitude to the man who had saved my life. Although Mr. A loved to talk, he was also a good listener and only interrupted when he needed something specific explained.

When I got to the part where I had figured out that Julien Floyd was the criminal, I said, "Visiting your antique shop to interview you came with an extra benefit. From that day on, everything was clear to me, even though I couldn't prove it."

"I don't follow."

"Amid other, unrelated items in your shop, I noticed a brass desk lamp mounted on a marble base. That lamp did the trick for me! It reminded me of a comment that Julien made twice. He said that Jake may have been absent-minded and placed the ammonium nitrate too close to the heat lamp. He couldn't have known about any ammonium nitrate or a heat lamp being in his colleague's laboratory unless he was the culprit."

Mr. A grinned as he asked, "So one of my treasures helped you solve the crime?"

"Absolutely," I stated.

CHAPTER 48

On Sunday morning, I got a phone call from the people at Oma's nursing home and was told that she was fading. I dropped everything and drove to Pasadena.

The caregiver met me at the reception desk and said, "Your grandmother has been confined to her bed in the last two days. She's too weak to get up, I'm sorry to say. Our PR person has the day off today, but she'll contact your folks to let them know about her current condition first thing tomorrow morning."

I said, "There's no need for her to do that, I'll let my parents know myself."

The caregiver then said, "You may go to her room; she's resting comfortably. I told her you were coming but am not sure whether she understood."

I entered Oma's room and found her stretched out on the bed, staring at the ceiling. Her face held an anemic pallor and her neck bones jutted out like spikes. Beneath the sheet, the contours of her body appeared to be those of a child. For a moment, I had a hard time keeping my composure, seeing my once vibrant Oma shriveled down to this small bundle of misery. For her sake, I pulled myself together and stepped closer.

Kissing her on both cheeks, I said cheerfully, "So what's this business of sleeping in?"

Slowly her eyes shifted away from the ceiling and focused on me. She smiled and exclaimed, "Rubin!"

I was about to explain that the nickname Rubin was her daughter's and that I was Tara, her granddaughter, then decided to skip setting her straight. I could be Rubin if she wanted me to be.

I said, "Sorry that we can't walk around the garden and look at your favorite things."

Then I had an idea and announced, "Hold on, Oma. I'll be right back," and darted out of the room.

On the nursing home's grounds, I took several photos with my smart phone and then rushed back to her.

Once I had her attention again, I announced, "Let's take our walk through the garden now," and I showed her the picture of the hummingbird feeder. Next I scrolled to the one of the water fountain.

She said, "Splash."

"Yes," I agreed. "It makes a splashing sound."

When I showed her the picture of the sunflowers, Oma touched the photo and smiled.

I glided my finger to the last image and suggested, "Let's sit down on your favorite bench and I'll tell you a story."

Knowing that she might only understand a fraction of what I was about to tell her but would enjoy listening to my voice, I started with, "This is a continuation of my playing at being a detective. I told you about it last time I was here and also the time before then. When I saw you a week ago, you said something that helped me a great deal. Remember what that was?"

She did not reply, and I said, "You told me the words, 'go back.' As I drove home after seeing you, it suddenly occurred to me that Julien must have *gone back* to Jake's guesthouse once more in the late afternoon on the day of the explosion. So you see, all the puzzle pieces fell into place from then on, and it was all thanks to you!"

She smiled but kept quiet and I went on to tell her the entire development of events since I had seen her last. I elaborated on my visiting Julien's new lab and how I confronted him with his crimes, which ultimately led to his confession. I described the previous day's bomb scare in my apartment and ended with my experience of giving evidence to the detectives at the police station.

I added, "Mr. A saved my life. In the future, I'll never try to sneak by his door undetected again. Instead, I'll listen patiently to his gabs. And after getting home today, I'll start working on the column about his antique shop, making sure to say lots of nice things about it."

"Nice things," Oma repeated.

"Can you believe I almost fell for a killer? Oh, he could let out the charm if it suited him. I felt his magnetism from the day I first met him at the banquet held in his honor. Now it makes me sick to think back to the clever speech he gave at the event. He talked about the tragic passing of his friend and colleague, Dr. Jake Unger, saying that he knew that Jake was in the final stages of his own findings and would have contributed his version to the contest, had he survived. And then he had the gall to have the assembled join him in a moment of silence for his friend."

I shuddered with disgust and then stayed silent for a while. Oma soon closed her eyes, and I could tell that I had exhausted her. I gave her one last hug, then tiptoed out of the room.

CHAPTER 49

As soon as I got home, I called Mom.

She said, "Your Dad has been home for a few days now and seems back to normal. At least his motorcycle has been stationary in the garage ever since. I'll put you on speaker."

Dad came on the line and I asked, "How was New Orleans?"

"Great, and so were all the other towns I rode through. I had a blast, but it's good to be back. Like the saying goes, 'There's no place like home!'"

"I'm glad you got it out of your system, Dad."

"So what's new with you?"

"Not much, other than I solved a murder and hope that the killer will be brought to justice in due course."

Mom cried out, "What's that you said about a murder?"

"It's a long story. I'll tell it all in person someday."

"Have you put yourself in danger, Tara?"

"Not anymore," I stated, laughing with relief.

Then I became somber and said, "I just came back from Pasadena. Oma is extremely frail and bedridden. The nursing home people planned to call you, but I said I'd let you know myself."

Mom said, "Thank you for being good to her."

"Oma thought I was you, and I left her the illusion."

"Thank you for that too!"

"You'd best drive down soon, if you want to see her alive."

"Oh, she's that bad? We'll get down to see her next weekend and stop by at Huntington Beach to pay you a visit too," Mom assured me.

Oma died in her sleep three days later. Mom and Dad did not make it down to see her alive. They only were in time for her funeral.

CHAPTER 50

The trial was held on Monday, December 10 of that year. As I had expected, there existed a remote storage file of Dr. Unger's data regarding his intended entry to the Tops & Associates contest. This had been easy for the authorities to investigate and verify, and it was added as another piece of concrete evidence. The substantial evidence was, however, what they had found when searching Julien Floyd's apartment. He had been too cocky and sure of himself to get rid of the reflex hammer he had used on Jake. The search of his place also revealed traces of the substance he had used to make the bomb meant for me.

Several witnesses for the prosecution were called to testify, i.e. Brenda Unger, Rob Cloud, the CEO of Tops & Associates, and the police officer who had caught Julien red-handed attaching the explosive device to my air-conditioning duct.

But, as one can imagine, I was the main witness called. I had never testified in court before and did not enjoy the experience. Not only had Julien glared at me menacingly during my entire time on the stand, but his defense attorney grilled me relentlessly on cross examination. The idea was to get me to contradict myself, but he did not succeed. Still, I left the witness box drained and exhausted.

There were three witnesses for the defense. One was a former boss of Julien who insisted that the accused was more than capable of arriving at a solution for the contest on his own and wouldn't have resorted to stealing it. Next was a psychiatrist who claimed that Julien had been verbally and mentally abused by his parents while growing up, leaving him with a constant urge to prove himself. The third was a character witness, Julien's landlady, testifying that her tenant was a charming, respectable, and soft-spoken man who wouldn't hurt a fly, let alone a human being.

The jury evidently could not be swayed by any of that and convicted Dr. Julien Floyd of several felonies: fraud, grand theft, the murder of Dr. Jake Unger, breaking and entering, and the attempted murder of Tara Blunt.

The sentencing followed days later. Julien was condemned to life in prison. In addition, the late Dr. Unger was declared the rightful winner of the contest and the prize money, plus the trip for two to Paris, France - - both of which were awarded to his widow. In other words, Julien had to give the millions back, including liquidating his new lab and handing over the Paris trip.

EPILOGUE

There are a few loose ends that need to be addressed. Isn't that what epilogues are for in conventional books?

I was curious and called my friend Max, the life insurance agent, to inquire who ended up collecting Jake Unger's life insurance money. He told me that it had been the most unusual case he had ever come across. Since there had been no written request to make a change to the policy naming Brenda Unger as the beneficiary, theoretically, Konrad König stood to benefit. But these were special circumstances.

According to Max, there had been a documented phone call from Jake to the insurance company on the day before the explosion and also his statement to Konrad König on the actual day, leaving no doubt that he intended to make his request in writing. In fact, it was likely that the piece of mail sat in Jake's lab, ready to be mailed, on that very day. In that case, the request would have been destroyed by the fire.

Consequently, all three parties, the insurance company, Konrad König, and Brenda Unger had put their heads together, and it was agreed upon to split the life insurance money between Jake Unger's widow and the leader of Astute.

On a Thursday morning in March of the next year, I ran into Brenda at the gym. We were both done with our workouts and sat down in the gym's lobby to chat.

She said, "After the trial, I wanted to thank you for all you did to get justice for Jake but never got around to it." She smiled and stated, "So I'm thanking you now."

"No thanks are necessary," I assured her.

Then I remarked, "I'm surprised to find you still in the area."

She was quick to get my meaning and said, "You thought I'd cash in my millions and move on."

"Something like that," I admitted.

"To tell the truth, I was thinking of divorcing Jake before he died. Then, when all that contest money of his came my way, I felt guilty as hell. I ended up giving half of it to Rob Cloud and also the equipment that was left from Julien Floyd's new lab."

"How generous of you!"

"As I said, I did it out of guilt. I figured that Rob can use the money for scientific research, and who knows, he may even discover some major breakthrough. I'm sure Jake would've wanted it that way."

I saw the man, his tiny ponytail sticking straight up, clearly in my mind. Rob Cloud may have been socially awkward, but I could well imagine that he was a talented scientist.

I remarked, "I'm positive he's putting the money to good use." Then I asked, "How are things going otherwise?"

She had not missed my glance in the direction of her ring finger and said, "Yes, Jeff and I are engaged. We're having the wedding at the end of May. I wanted to wait at least a year after - - you know - -"

I nodded in understanding.

She continued, "Jeff is good with Logan. It'll work out."

"Well, congratulations, and I wish you, Logan, and Jeff the best."

She hesitated for a second, then shared, "Jeff suggested we use the trip to Paris for our honeymoon, but I can't bring myself to do that. Jake won it, and I'd feel shamefaced to go there with Jeff. I haven't decided yet what I'll do with it."

Before we parted I asked, "I'm curious, what happened with your house? Is it yours and yours only, or has Bryan Unger found a way to make you sell it?"

"That battle is still unsettled. Bryan is taking me to court over it," she replied.

A few days later, to my great surprise, I found a short letter from Brenda in the mail. It read:

"Dear Tara,

"I may not always have shown it, but I appreciate all that you have done. Jake was a good man and deserved justice. I finally thought of a way to thank you.

Enjoy the attached!

Brenda."

Enclosed was the trip for two to Paris.

I knew just whom to ask to come along. My friend Crystal had been going through rough times again. It turned out that her Mr. Wonderful also had a Mrs. Wonderful. My friend could use some distraction and fun times. Staying at a five star hotel in Paris, visiting the sites, and enjoying a bit of nightlife might do the trick.

Once a month, I visit Oma at Forest Lawn. More often than not, I place a sunflower or two on her grave. The last time I dropped by, the following popped into my head, "Go back!" What did you really mean with those words, Oma? They served me well in my investigation. But what had you tried to tell me? Had you grasped the essence of my detective story and, in an instant of clear thinking, pointed out the simple fact that Julien went back to the Ungers' guesthouse in the afternoon? Or could it be that you were informing me that soon you'll be going back to your Maker? I guess I'll never know.

As for me, solving a crime provided some satisfaction, but it also was tedious and exhausting work. I did not mind the danger as much as all it had taken out of me. In short, I was living and breathing the investigation. From day one, the thing fell into my lap, and once I started, I could no longer let it go. I'm thinking back to that Saturday morning on April 14 of last year, when it all began as I landed my interview with Jake Unger. Well, Dr. Unger, you won that contest, there is no more denying that!

If I could re-live my life from that day in April onward, what would I change?

Not a single thing!

Stand-Alone Mysteries by Alice Zogg

The Ill-Fated Scientist

Accidental Eyewitness

A Bet Turned Deadly

R. A. Huber Mysteries by Alice Zogg

Evil at Shore Haven

Guilty or Not

Murder at the Cubbyhole

Revamp Camp

Final Stop Albuquerque

The Fall of Optimum House

The Lonesome Autocrat

Tracking Backward

Turn the Joker Around

Reaching Checkmate

www.ingramcontent.com/pod-product-compliance
Lightning Source LLC
Chambersburg PA
CBHW030322180626
46810CB00003B/1196